CHRISTMASLAND

A SWEET, SMALL TOWN CHRISTMAS ROMANCE

ANNE-MARIE MEYER

For every Emilia out there

BEATRICE

"**M**erry Christmas!" the street vendor yelled into my face just as I walked past him.

He shoved a snow globe in my direction, and I stepped back right into a puddle of melted snow mixed with the runoff of New York City streets. I yelped and leapt forward, nearly taking out a group of women who were perusing the exact item that could have nearly killed me.

I gave them a sheepish smile, but they just glared at me. They returned to whispering and moving the snow globes around in their hands as if by rubbing the glass hard enough, they'd be transported to the clean and crisp depictions of a Christmas town.

I snorted. The only place such a town existed was in Christmas decorations and your imagination.

"Well?" the vendor asked as he waved the snow globe under my nose.

I studied him. Was he serious? Did he really think that I was going to buy something from him when my foot was soaked and freezing? I was pretty sure I was halfway to either getting a foot fungus or frostbite.

"I'm good," I said as I lifted up my mittened hands and began to back away.

"Your loss," he shouted after me as I hurried away from him.

"Yeah, right," I said as I spotted the Java Bean and veered toward it. This was the last time I was going to let Em pick our coffee spot for the week. Next time, we were going to Buzzed. It was a block down from my apartment and wasn't surrounded by all of this Christmas cheer.

I wasn't exactly what you would call a grinch, but there was only so much tinsel, cinnamon, and Santa a girl could take. My holly-jolly meter was pretty much full, and it was only the first week of December.

I reached the front door of Java Bean and had to wait as a group of sufficiently buzzed patrons exited. They were laughing and talking. From what I could tell, they were talking about their Christmas plans. I held the door open for them, using the polite gesture to eavesdrop.

As a writer, I got my ideas from everywhere. So what if I used my goodwill to my advantage? They got the door opened for them, and I got material to use for the next chapter of my book.

That was what I called a win-win.

Once inside, I slipped off my pink beanie and shoved it into my jacket pocket. I attempted to smooth down my curly brown hair, but, with the mixture of static and my wiry hair, the effort was in vain. I ended up looking like Einstein's granddaughter.

I heard Em's easy laugh and spotted her red hair in the corner of the shop. After placing my very boring order of black coffee with two sugars, I made my way over and plopped down across from her.

She'd just finished taking a drink of something very Christmassy and very frothy. When she lowered her mug, there was a line of whipped cream above her lip. She saw me and smiled but didn't move to wipe away the remnants of her drink.

"Em," I said as my OCD went into hyperdrive. I grabbed a nearby napkin and reached over to wipe off the froth.

"I got it. I got it." She giggled as she took the napkin from my hand and wiped her mouth. "I'm so glad to have you as my mother."

I snorted as I sat back down in my chair and glanced around. Although I knew Em was joking, there was always a sadness that rose up inside of me at the mention of parents. I was one of the lucky products of the foster care system. Even though I was grateful that I had foster parents who cared about me, this time of year only made my loneliness more poignant.

Not wanting to be the downer at the table, I changed the subject. "Why did you drag me down here?" I motioned toward my water-stained suede boots and darkened pant leg.

Em laughed. "What happened to you?"

I glared at her. "It's not funny. I was basically assaulted by a man selling snow globes. In order to avoid his clutches, I had to jump back into a lovely puddle of melted snow and gunk."

Em wrinkled her nose for a moment before she waved off my comment. "I like it here. There is Christmas everywhere. Unlike your apartment, which looks like a hospital room." She cupped her mug with both hands and brought the rim to her nose, taking in a deep breath. She closed her eyes as if it were the most exquisite thing in the world.

"You are hopelessly optimistic," I said as I sighed. Em lived and breathed Christmas.

"Oh," she said so loudly that it startled me.

I clutched my hand to my chest and gave her an exasperated look. "What the heck?"

If Em heard me, she didn't say anything. Instead, she leaned forward with her eyes sparkling from excitement.

"Beatrice Thompson, you are not going to believe what I won this morning."

Realizing that she hadn't startled me for a life-threatening reason, I settled back against my chair and thanked the barista as she brought me my drink. I picked up the bottle of cream from the middle of the table and poured it in.

I knew my hesitancy to be as excited as Em was would bother her, but I didn't care. It was our time-honored tradition. She got excited, and I remained calm. There was no way I was going to start changing things now.

"Bea," she whined as she dipped down to meet my gaze.

I brought my coffee to my lips and took a sip only to have the flavor of mint coat my tongue. "Bleh." I'd just poured some mint-flavored cream into my coffee. Great.

No longer wanting my drink, I set it off to the side and then rested my elbows on the table and my chin in my palms. "All right, tell me."

She smiled—a bit too bright—as she leaned in. "I won…" She paused as she glanced around as if the beanie-wearing man on our left or the group of high school girls to our right were trying their best to eavesdrop. "Two tickets to Christmasland."

I blinked once and then twice as her words set in. "Did you just say Christmasland?"

Em pinched her lips together as she nodded. "Christmasland," she whispered.

I reached down and pinched my leg. My best friend had actually said *Christmasland* as if that were a place that actually existed. As a sharp pain shot through my leg, I realized that this was not a nightmare but real life.

"I'm pretty sure there isn't a place called Christmasland," I said as I reached out and fiddled with the traitorous cream bottle. Why did everything have to be festive? Why couldn't we just leave cream alone? Not everything had to have a holiday line.

"It so does exist. And I can't wait for us to go." She leaned back in her chair as she sipped on her drink.

"I'm sorry, we?"

Em smiled, but she must have seen my hesitation. Suddenly

she was leaning in with a desperate look in her eye. "Come on, Bea. This is a once-in-a-lifetime experience. It's an all-paid trip to Vermont. We get to stay at the North Pole and participate in all of the festivities of Christmasland."

I patted my cheeks and moved to stand. "I need to wake up," I said.

"Wait!" She grasped at my arm in an attempt to get me to stay. Not wanting her to knock over the table just to keep me from leaving, I sat down.

I folded my arms as I studied her. I was ready for her to start making sense.

She took in a deep breath as she steepled her hands in front of her. She touched her lips with her forefingers. I could tell she was taking her time to find the right words.

"Think of it like this. It's a four-day, five-night stay at an all-inclusive bed and breakfast. There are festivities that you can participate in" —I raised my eyebrows— "or not," she amended. "You don't have to participate." Her quick change of course caused me to smile.

At least my best friend knew me. Silence fell around our table as I started chewing on what she'd said. An all-paid *anything* sounded amazing. I was trying to be a writer but failing. The only thing that was keeping me off the streets was my job as a bank teller. Jonathan, my boss, had just been telling me that if I didn't take my vacation days, they would disappear at the start of the new year.

So maybe this could work out.

I heard Em squeal. When I looked up at her, she covered her lips with her hand, but I could see her glee. I took in a deep breath.

"All right," I said slowly, "I'll go to Christmasland with you."

She yelped, causing the beanie-wearing guy next to us to jump. He glared at her, and she offered him an apologetic smile.

"I'm sorry," she whispered and then turned to me where she tried to stifle her giggle but was failing horribly.

I thought about taking back my offer. I considered backing out. But Em looked so happy. Her family would be overseas this holiday season, and she was just as alone as I was—I couldn't take away her happiness. Not when I had no good reason other than that it wasn't really my thing.

So I gave her a forced smile and pumped my fists in the air. She clapped her hands together and started in on everything we were going to do and how excited she was. I tried to look just as excited, but I knew that I was failing miserably.

All I needed to do was survive, and I would be okay. That was all I needed to do.

Survive.

2

ETHAN

I couldn't believe I'd agreed to this. There was no way I got in my car and drove the twenty-odd hours to Vermont just to stand outside of Mom's overly decorated house in Christmasland. I should have just checked myself into the psych ward at one of the many hospitals I'd driven by on my way here.

"I'm insane," I whispered as I climbed out of my car. The snow crunched under my boots. I took in a deep breath in an effort to prepare myself for what was going to come my way. A whole lot of Christmas cheer wrapped up in the form of my mother.

When Dad died fifteen years ago, Mom spiraled. She began to stock their historical house full of Christmas items. Where I saw clutter, Mom saw a business opportunity. Soon, her house was packed full of people who wanted the taste of Christmas.

I was still shocked that she'd managed to get the whole town in on it, but they'd seen her vision and leaned into it. The result of Mom's entrepreneurship was Christmasland. An entire town dedicated to the spirit of Christmas.

And I'd somehow let Mom talk me into coming back. I was officially off my rocker.

I grabbed my suitcase and computer bag from the trunk and

then slammed it shut. I walked across the back yard and pulled open the door that led into the kitchen. Warmth and the mouth-watering smells of roast and fresh baked bread filled my nose instantly, making my salivary glands perk up.

I may not have missed Mom's knickknacks, but I'd definitely missed Mom's cooking.

A low, deep bark drew my attention up. I stomped my feet to release the snow and smiled at Rudolph, who had perked up from his bed in the corner. His once vibrant, Saint Bernard coat had now dulled, and the hair around his nose was feathered with white.

"Hush, Rudolph." Mom's voice sounded from around the corner. I slipped off my shoes and left my suitcase and bag by the door.

"Hey, Ma," I said as I came up next to her.

Mom was in the middle of stirring some gravy, and at first, it didn't look like she registered who I was. But the moment passed, and suddenly Mom was squealing and moving to pull me into one of her crushing hugs. She was a tiny woman but formidable. And she gave the best hugs.

"My baby's come home," she whispered as she held me tight.

I hugged her back, but she didn't seem interested in letting me go. My back was cricked from bending forward, and I felt a tad smothered. Since I had missed her as much as it seemed she missed me, I let her hug me for as long as she needed.

When she pulled back, I noticed that her eyes were misty, and that caused the lump in my throat to grow. She was lonely, and I'd been the jerk son that had stayed away.

"It's good to see you, too."

She reached up and patted my cheek with her hand. Then a moment later, a spark glistened in her eye, and suddenly, she was pushing me toward the small round table in the corner by Rudolph. She put pressure on my shoulders until I sat.

"Let me get you some food," she said as she hurried back into the kitchen and pulled down a plate.

"Ma," I responded, but she just waved it away.

Realizing that there was no way I could sway her from what she wanted to do, I settled back in my seat and let my stress start to melt away. Even though the house was more cluttered than I preferred, it still felt like...home.

When Mom returned, she set down a plate heaped with food —meat, potatoes, roasted green beans, all of it slathered in gravy. After she handed me some utensils, she hurried off only to return with a basket full of warm rolls.

She settled next to me and watched as I started eating. It was awkward to have her studying me so intently. I gave her a small smile.

"Why don't you eat with me?" I asked as I motioned toward my plate.

Mom shook her head. "I already ate. Plus, it's getting hard to fit into my pants." She giggled as her cheeks flushed. Then she leaned in. "Too many Christmas cookies."

Mom made incredible cookies. She'd won quite a few awards at the county fairs.

We kept our conversation light as I finished up my plate. Once the food was gone, I pushed the plate away and leaned back, trying to make room for my stomach. It had been a long time since I felt this full from a meal. It was nice, even if it hurt just a bit.

"Good?" Mom asked as she stood to take my plate.

I motioned for her to sit and then stood to take my plate over to the sink and rinse it off. After I loaded it into the dishwasher, I turned to see that Mom had come into the kitchen to join me. She poured two mugs of coffee and handed me one. I took it, but when she offered me some holiday flavored cream, I waved it off.

"I'm good. I'll just stick with sugar."

"Still resisting the flavored creamers?" she asked. Her tease only accented her smile.

"Why mess with something that's already good?" I brought the mug to my lips and took a sip.

"When you add Christmas to something, it doesn't mess it up. Look at this town. Adding Christmas revived it." She tapped her nose. "We created a magical world in the middle of the mundane."

I studied Mom as she spoke. She was truly happy. This was what she was meant to do. Jealousy crept up inside of me. I wished I felt the same. I wasn't sure what I was meant to do, and no matter what I did, I never felt confident that my decisions were right.

I reached out and wrapped my arm around Mom's shoulders. I brought her in and gave her a quick squeeze. She smiled and patted my hand, and we stood there in silence. Even though I'd fought coming back, I was glad I did.

A moment later, Mom sighed and turned to face me. "You know that there is no such thing as a free meal," she said as she narrowed her eyes. Sweet Mom had disappeared, and suddenly, business woman took her place.

I should have known this would happen.

"What do you have in mind?" I asked as I stepped over to the counter and leaned against it. I folded my arms and stretched out my legs in front of me.

Mom gave me a wicked smile as she drummed her fingers on the countertop. "A lot."

Perhaps I should have run away as soon as Mom's Cheshire-cat smile emerged, or when she declared that I'd be working as her elf and showed me to the empty room I was going to stay in. But I didn't.

Instead, I decided that, no matter what, leaving wasn't an option. I was going to stick around here until after the holidays. Then I would decide what I was going to do, and I'd stick to it. If that meant going back to Chicago, then I'd go. If it meant staying here...well, I'd make the decision when the time came.

For now, I was going to drown myself in work and try to survive all of this holiday cheer.

That's what I'd been doing most of my life—trying to survive.

3

BEATRICE

I was not going to survive. I'd been a fool to agree to this, and
as I stood outside of my apartment building with my suitcase tucked in next to me and the cold winter air whipping
around me, I contemplated running back upstairs and hiding
under my covers. Em would survive without me. After all, she
was fun and outgoing. She'd make a new best friend who liked
eggnog and holiday flavored coffee creamer.

Maybe it was for the best. She could move on with someone
who enjoyed all the things she did, and I could lean into the
hermit lifestyle that I seemed destined to live out. Why should I
fight the inevitable?

I wrapped my fingers around the handle of my suitcase, and
just as I started to turn, I heard a loud and persistent honk.
Glancing down the road, I saw Em's bright-blue Volkswagen Bug
as it cut off a Camry. She pulled up to the curb and jumped out.

"Where are you going?" she asked as she rounded the hood.
There was some freshly fallen snow on the road, and in her haste,
she lost her footing for a moment. Desperate to keep from falling
flat, she grabbed at the hood of her car.

It was like watching a slow-motion movie. I stepped forward

to help her, but I was still a good ten feet away. Thankfully, she was able to catch herself and a moment later was upright again.

I raised my eyebrows as she offered me a perky smile. Her cheeks were flushed, but there was a twinkle in her eye. She was excited, and there was no way I wanted to take that away from her.

"I'm okay. I'm okay," she said as she hurried over to me.

"It seems like a bad omen." I held onto my suitcase for a moment, but Em was more determined than I was and eventually yanked it from my grasp.

"No, it's not. It's actually good luck," she called over her shoulder as she made her way to the trunk.

"Falling on your butt in the snow is good luck?"

"It is," she yelled as she disappeared into the trunk. I heard her shuffle things around, and then a moment later, she popped back up as she slammed the trunk closed. "All set," she sang out.

I took in a deep breath. This was fine. I was fine. I could do this. After all, it was just for a few days.

Em had sent me close to a hundred emails depicting what we were going to do at Christmasland. I think she feared I was going to back out and wanted to get me excited. Her emails did nothing of the sort. Instead, they freaked me out.

Christmasland was a small town in Vermont. Apparently, the entire town had transformed into the embodiment of every holiday cliché. They didn't give a lot of details about what they do, just that you are "guaranteed the quintessential Christmas experience."

Lord help me.

I dragged my feet a bit more, but Em wasn't having it. She hurried over and hooked arms with me. She pulled me toward the passenger side of the car and shoved me inside.

Once we were on the road, I tried to relax, but that seemed far-fetched. I was pretty sure I was going to spend the entire trip as a jumble of nerves. Thankfully I had writing to do, and from what Em said, she'd been given the master suite at the North Pole bed and breakfast. The perfect place to rejigger my creative juices and get the inspiration flowing again.

I was stuck in my story, and I feared I would never get out of it.

I leaned against my headrest and listened as Em rattled on about what we were going to do. Christmas music played softly in the background, and as I stared out the window, watching the snow-covered world pass by, I actually began to relax.

I wasn't going to have work or the stress of living in the city for the next few days. I might as well enjoy that freedom even if it came with a town full of people who thought I loved Christmas as much as they did.

"Fifteen miles away!" Em sang out as we passed the sign for Christmasland.

I glanced over at her as she tightened her grip on the steering wheel, and a crazed smile passed over her face.

"Calm down," I said as I shifted to sit up in my seat. Trees spanned out in both directions. They were covered with white snow, and with the sun shining down, it made the world feel brighter. I had to admit it helped my mood.

Suddenly, the sound of something exploding mixed with the car jerking to the left had us both screaming. Em took charge, pulled the car onto the shoulder, and threw the car into park.

My heart was pounding as I took in deep breaths. When I glanced over at Em, she looked as terrified as I did.

"Are you okay?" I asked.

She nodded and turned to stare at me. Her eyes were wide, and for a moment, she looked worried until her lips tipped up into a...smile? "It's starting."

I blinked. "What?"

She giggled as she hurried to unbuckle her seatbelt and climbed out of the car. I moved to follow her until we were both standing in front of the flat tire. Em was giggling, and my brain was still trying to process why she was so giddy.

"Em, your tire is flat. Doesn't that bother you?" My breath swirled around my head as I spoke.

Em shook her head. "You haven't seen many Hallmark movies, have you?"

"Hallmark movies?"

Em nodded fervently. "From the blogs and videos I've seen of this place, they put you into situations just like the movies." She waved her hand toward her tire.

My best friend had officially gone insane. "You think the town purposely popped your tire so that you can, what, be saved by some handsome stranger?"

Em squealed as she gripped onto my arm and jumped up and down. "Yes."

"You're crazy," I said as I pulled away from her and headed over to the trunk. "We just need to change the tire and then get you to a mechanic, so we can buy a new tire just like every normal human." After digging around in the trunk, I found the spare and the jack.

Em was no help. Instead she stood there, peering down the road.

"Are you not going to help me?" I asked as I gingerly knelt down in the compacted snow and then placed my hands on the ground to peer under the car.

"I'm telling you, this is all part of the experience," she called from above me.

"That is insane. You know that, right?"

It took me a hot minute, but I was able to find a flat surface to place the jack under. I cheered myself on as I straightened and began pumping the handle to raise the car. I glanced over at Em, who was blowing into her hands. She was bouncing up and down on her feet as she kept her post.

"No one's coming," I said as I finished raising the car. I stood and walked over to her. She glanced at me.

"They are."

I loved my friend, but I hated her unwavering faith. She knew that someone was coming. I knew they weren't. If I trusted in what she'd said, we would end up as two human popsicles on the side of the road.

"Well, you keep a lookout, and I'll keep fixing the tire."

Just as I turned back to the car, movement down the road drew my attention. A truck was coming over the hill, and as I squinted to see better, I realized that it was a tow truck.

Em cheered, and suddenly my arm was being yanked back and forth. "See, I told you."

This had to be a coincidence. After all, there was no way a town was out popping people's tires just so they could rescue them. I could only imagine the legal battles that would ensue from something like this.

"This isn't—"

"It's part of the experience." Em gave me a look that said, *don't ruin this for me.*

So I pinched my lips together and nodded. If she wanted to believe that blowing a tire and having a tow truck miraculously show up to rescue us was part of her Christmasland vacation, I'd let her.

The tow truck slowed as it pulled in behind our car. It idled for a moment before the driver's door opened, and we saw two feet land on the ground. The door slammed, revealing the driver's dark eyes and dark curly hair. He was wearing a flannel button-down shirt with a light-brown jacket. He furrowed his brow as he glanced from me to Em.

"Need some help?" he asked.

"Wow," Em whispered. Then she turned to me. *All part of the experience*, she mouthed.

My cheeks heated as the man furrowed his brow. Desperate to

make sure he didn't think we were crazy people, I stepped away from Em and up to him. That was a stupid mistake. Even though there was no way I believed that this was somehow part of Christmasland, I knew a good-looking man when I saw one.

And this man was good-looking in a rugged, mysterious way. Just as I moved to stand next to him, the wind picked up and surrounded me with his cologne. It smelled like the mountains after a summer rain. If there was such a way to bottle that scent up and sell it.

"You okay?" the man asked. He leaned forward and suddenly appeared in my line of sight.

I blinked a few times and nodded. "Yeah."

He didn't look convinced, but he also didn't seem interested in pushing it. "I can give you a tow if you need it."

"We're headed to Christmasland," Em piped up from behind me. She must have overcome her stupor and was ready to join the real world. "Are you from there?"

The man nodded. "Yeah."

"Interesting," she said, more for me than for him.

He looked confused, but that didn't last long. "So, is that a yes?"

"That's a yes..." Em leaned in, and it took the man a moment before he realized what she was expecting from him.

"Ethan."

"It's nice to meet you, Ethan." She elbowed me as if his name should elicit some excitement. "I'm Emilia, and this is Beatrice. But you can call me Em and her Bea."

Ethan glanced between us. I felt like an idiot, but it seemed as if his gaze lingered a few seconds longer on me. Then I pushed that thought from my mind.

This was *not* a Hallmark movie, and he was not the main love interest.

We climbed into the cab of his truck and waited as he hooked up the car. I was stuck in the middle between Em and the empty driver's seat. I was trying to prepare myself for him inevitably sitting next to me.

It seemed simple enough, and I was fairly certain there was no reason I should feel nervous...but I did. And I hated that.

"Isn't this fun?" Em asked as she paused her humming to link arms with me and squeeze.

My friend had officially gone insane.

But I knew she was excited, so I nodded. "Yes."

Ten minutes passed before Ethan climbed into the cab. He squeezed in next to me as he pulled the door closed. My heart rate picked up speed as I tried to shush it. After all, I wasn't going to be put into the same category as Em. She was crazy, and I was sane.

At least, that was how I wanted to come across.

Ethan glanced over at us as he started the engine. Every time he moved, he brushed against me, and my entire body warmed from the touch. So when he met my gaze, I forced myself to appear cool and collected.

"Ready?" he asked.

We both nodded, and he pulled back out onto the road.

The only sound that filled the silence between us was Em humming under her breath. I thought about talking but feared what I might say, so I kept my arms folded and my lips pinched shut. I was ready to get to the North Pole and relax.

Ethan took a left, and a few seconds later, the site of a small, ridiculously decorated town came into view. The buildings were painted all different colors, and there were string lights everywhere.

The speed changed to thirty, and Ethan slowed. As we approached the town, he glanced over at us and said exactly what the sign we'd just passed said, "Welcome to Christmasland."

4

BEATRICE

Of all the things that I imagined Christmasland to be, there was no way I could have imagined what I was currently seeing. It was like I'd gone from the real world to living in a snow globe. Or one of those Christmas towns that grandmothers spent their entire life collecting.

Everything was decorated for Christmas. The light poles were wrapped in tinsel and greenery. And I was fairly certain when darkness came, this town would be so bright, you could see it from outer space.

People milled around on the sidewalks. You could tell the difference between the locals and the tourists. The residents were decked out head to toe in different combinations of red and green. They also wore ridiculously wide smiles as they talked to the normally dressed patrons.

This was going to be interesting.

Ethan drove past, not bothering to speak or explain what we were seeing. If his job was to welcome us to the town, he was doing a poor job. I took a moment to peek over at him. He wasn't dressed like the other people in town. Did he live here? Or was he just passing through?

I parted my lips to ask him, but before I could get a word out, he waved toward the mechanic shop on our left. "Here we are," he said as he pulled in and put the truck into park.

Before either of us could respond, he'd jumped out and slammed the door.

I glanced over at Em, who was staring at me with wide eyes. I frowned. "What?" There was no way I liked how she was looking at me.

"I didn't say anything."

I sighed. "Yeah, but you look like you are holding something back. Spill it."

Her lips continued to creep up until she was grinning at me. "It's exactly like the movies. A brooding townsperson with a grinch-like heart. All he needs is a stranger to change his mind." She wiggled her eyebrows.

Worried my friend was actually having a stroke, I reached out and pressed my hand to her forehead. "Are you sure you are feeling alright?"

She swatted my hand away. "You jest, but eventually you'll find out I'm right." Then she tapped her chin. "That questionnaire finally makes sense."

My entire body froze. "Questionnaire? I didn't fill out a questionnaire."

Em didn't look bothered as she smoothed out her jacket and glanced over at me. "I filled it out for you."

"What? What did you say?"

She narrowed her eyes. "On a scale of one to jolly, I said you were a one in terms of holiday spirit."

A feeling of dread filled my chest. "Why would you say that?"

Em looked innocent as she studied me. "They want to give you a personalized experience." Then she grinned. "I said that I was a Cindy Lou Who."

I stared at her.

"You know, from the movie *How the Grinch Stole Christmas?*

She wants to find the true meaning of Christmas. Except I already know the meaning."

My friend had officially jumped off the deep end. I'd known her most of my life, but I'd never seen this part of her.

"So, what are they going to do to me?"

Em chuckled. "You make it sound like they are going to murder you." She patted my knee. "Don't be scared. It'll be fun, and by the end, I'm sure you'll love Christmas as much as I do."

I wanted her to take that back. In fact, I had half a mind to hijack this truck and head back to New York. After a few cleansing breaths, I decided that there was no need to commit a felony in order to get out of here. I could check into our room, and if I wanted to leave later, I would just call a cab…even if the ride back home would cost me my entire paycheck. I had options.

I wasn't a hostage to this town and their Christmas spirit. I could leave if I wanted to. That thought gave me some semblance of control.

A few minutes passed before Ethan pulled open the door and waved for us to get out.

"Oh," I said as I followed after Em.

Once we were on the ground, Ethan turned to face us. "Johnny is going to get your tire fixed."

"That's great," Em said and then elbowed me. "Isn't that great, Bea?"

I shot her a dirty look and then nodded and smiled at Ethan. "That's great."

Ethan studied the two of us for a moment before he nodded. "Great. Well, I guess I'll see you around."

"Yeah."

"Wait." Em reached out, her fingers lingering in the air just above Ethan's arm. "Could you give us a ride to the North Pole?"

Ethan's gaze dropped down to Em's hand and then back up. "You're going to the North Pole?"

Em nodded. "We won an all-inclusive package. We've got the master suite."

Ethan pulled out his keys and was fiddling with them. Then he sighed and nodded. "Well, that just happens to be where I'm going too."

"Really," Em said, purposely dragging out every letter as she glanced over at me. "That's quite a coincidence."

I wasn't sure what was going on, but the fact that Ethan not only had shown up to give us a tow but also just so happened to be going to our bed and breakfast...well, I was starting to wonder.

Then I shook my head to dislodge those thoughts. I wasn't going to go crazy like Em. I was going to stay levelheaded, and there was no way I was going to drink the Kool-Aid that was this town.

"Yeah." Ethan looked confused but seemed to brush it off. "Wanna get your bags? I'll pull my car around."

"Definitely." Em linked arms with me and started pulling me toward her car, which had just been lowered from the tow truck. After grabbing our bags, we made our way toward the street where Ethan had parked.

He was leaning against his car with his arms folded. I wasn't sure who he was looking at, but for a moment I wondered if he was looking at me. Heat flushed my skin as I chided myself. There was no way that I was going to become Em. There was nothing fishy going on here. Despite Em thinking that everything was orchestrated, I was going to choose to remain on the sane side of town.

The place where common sense lived.

We rolled our bags over to Ethan, who moved to help us load them into his car. Johnny the mechanic came over, handed Em an estimate for the repair, and told her that he'd call when the car was ready.

Em just nodded, took the paper from him, and shoved it into

her pocket. We climbed in Ethan's car, and he took off down the street.

The ride to the North Pole only took about ten minutes. My mouth dropped open as Ethan pulled up the winding driveway and stopped in front of a mansion. Every edge of the house was covered in lights. Fully decorated Christmas trees lined the wrap-around deck. A Saint Bernard with a bow for a collar lay on the top stair, his deep brown eyes peering down at us as we all climbed out.

I was fairly certain every tree around us was wrapped up in lights, and it made me wonder how well the drapes in our room worked. Would they be able to block out all the light coming in?

As we climbed out of the car and shut the doors, the dog sat up and let out a deep woof.

"Ah, be quiet, Rudolph," Ethan said as he waved his hand at the dog.

"Rudolph?" I asked as I met Ethan at the trunk.

He gave me a look that I couldn't quite read, but before I could delve into it, he opened the trunk and began pulling out the suitcases.

"Do you...do you live here?" I asked as Em came up behind me.

"Ha. No. I'm home for the holidays. I, um, live in Chicago."

Em nudged me with her elbow. "Big-city man coming home to his small town."

I pinched my lips as I turned to glare at her. There was no way I wanted Ethan to be a witness to this exchange.

"You're back!" Suddenly, a very plump woman appeared and wrapped her arms around Ethan. She had pure white hair and was wearing a bright red dress and a Christmas-print apron. When she pulled away, her gaze fell on us. "And who did you bring home with you?"

"Ma." Ethan leaned toward her. "These are the guests staying in Santa's suite."

My eyebrows rose at the name of the room.

"Ooo, the friends from New York. We've been expecting you."

"I'm Emilia, and this is Beatrice," Em said as she waved between us. I wasn't sure, but I swear I saw Em wink at the woman.

I didn't have time to process that thought because a moment later, the woman hurried over and grabbed my hand. Suddenly, I was being pulled across the driveway and up the front steps. "I am so excited that you are here," she said, pushing open the door and waving me inside.

"You are?" I asked as she ushered me into the foyer. It was like walking into the holiday section at a Target store. Every sort of decoration was out on display, but not in a tacky way. It made the home feel warmer, cozier.

Ethan's mom nodded. "You can call me Carol. Like Christmas carol." Her smile widened as if that were the funniest thing.

"Ah, okay."

After helping me take off my coat and hanging it on the antique coat rack by the door, she waved me over to the desk that sat at the base of the large staircase that cut the room in half.

She was riffling through papers as Em and Ethan came into the house and shut the door behind them. Em looked thrilled to be standing in the room. Her eyes kept darting around as if she were scared she would miss something.

Ethan looked unimpressed as he patted Rudolph's head and then started making his way toward the living room off to the left.

"Bags, Ethan," Carol called out.

He paused and slowly turned. He didn't look thrilled, but he didn't fight it. Instead, he grabbed our bags and started up the stairs. When he got midway, he glanced down at us. "Coming?"

I shoved my purse higher up onto my shoulder and started up the stairs. Carol handed Em the room keys, and she sprinted up after us. When we got to the top of the third flight of stairs, Ethan stood in front of the only door on the floor.

"Santa's suite," he said as Em unlocked the door and pushed it open.

Em screamed with joy as she entered the room. There was a fireplace on the left side. Next to it was a fully decorated Christmas tree. There was a plush couch in front of it and cookies on a plate sitting on the coffee table.

A large four-poster bed sat along the wall on the right. It was covered in fluffy pillows of all shades of red and green. A small train ran around the tree, and every few seconds, it blew its whistle.

I felt like I'd stepped into a Christmas movie.

"This is amazing," Em whispered.

"Well, I'll just leave you two to get settled," Ethan said as he set our bags down and then turned to leave.

For some reason, I wanted to say something to get him to stay, but nothing that made sense came to mind. So I just watched him walk out, shutting the door behind him. For a moment, I wondered if what Em had said was true. Was he the town's pick for me? Was he supposed to be the aloof guy to change my grinchy heart?

Ugh. I felt like an idiot.

Not wanting Em to see my shame, I made my way over to the bed and flung myself onto it, burying my face into the comforter. The fabric smelled like cinnamon and vanilla. Even the scents in the place were full of Christmas.

I flipped my head to the side and watched as she wandered around the room, sliding open drawers and looking out the window. She looked like a kid in a candy store. The only time she stopped was when she was standing in front of the Christmas tree where she let out a big sigh.

"What's wrong?" I turned to my side and rested my head on my hand.

"I was hoping that we were going to be able to pick and decorate a tree." She turned to face me with her hands on her hips. "But they already did it."

My gaze flicked over to the tree and then back to her. "I'm sure they could find another one for you to decorate."

Em dive-bombed the bed and then stretched out next to me. "I hope so." She lay on her back with her hands clasped and resting on her stomach. She sighed, and I saw her body begin to relax.

I moved to lie on my back as well, so we were both staring up at the ceiling. There was a chandelier above our bed with iridescent snowflakes painted all over.

"Are you happy?" I asked.

From the corner of my eye, I saw her nod. "I am. This is the epitome of Christmas, and I'm excited to start."

Even though I was hesitant to be here and had contemplated running away more than a few times, I was happy that my best friend was happy. "Well, my presence is your Christmas present, so…Merry Christmas."

Em reached out and patted my hand. "Merry Christmas to you, too." And then she squealed and buried her face in her hands.

I sighed as I turned my attention back up to the ceiling. I was going to be fine. I was. After all, it was just a few days, and then we'd be back home. I could survive a few days.

I could.

5

ETHAN

Christmasland

Mom looked suspicious as she stood at the bottom of the stairs. I eyed her and walked down until I was standing next to her. Her eyes were wide as if she were asking me a question, but I wasn't sure what that was.

Did she need an update on the status of the guests in Santa's suite? Or did she have something else in mind? Something much more sinister and most likely something I wanted no part of.

"How did it go?" she asked as I passed by her.

I gave her a look which I hoped would tell her to leave it alone, but she followed after me as I made my way into the kitchen. For the most part, Mom had left me alone to work these last few weeks. I fetched the wood, drove around guests, and cleaned rooms once they checked out.

We'd fallen into a system. But from the way she kept trying to catch my gaze, I was beginning to realize that our system was breaking down, and if I didn't intervene fast, it was going to disappear entirely.

"They are fine," I said as I pulled a water bottle from the fridge.

She tapped her chin, and I could see that she was trying to piece things together. "How did you know to pick them up?"

I took a long drink of water and then set the bottle down on the countertop. "I didn't. It was just a coincidence. Johnny asked if I could drop off a car for him in Stowe, and I told him I could. They were on the side of the road when I drove back." Then I furrowed my brow. "Why? Who are they?"

"Just the winners of the WKLZ competition. I was hoping to get some more publicity by hosting a raffle. So they need to enjoy themselves." Mom worried her lips as she paced around the kitchen.

"Why do you need more publicity?" The town was already packed full of tourists. I couldn't imagine that this town needed *more* people to fill it.

"I want to propose some new attractions to the city council in January, and if I can drum up excitement through the media, I think I'll have a greater chance of getting them to agree." She stopped pacing for a moment so that she could take a drink of her coffee. Then, she set the mug down and began moving again.

It made sense, but what confused me was Mom thinking that the girls weren't going to have a good time. Then I began to realize that something else was going on here.

"What did you do?"

Mom chuckled, but in a nervous way. That made my senses perk up even more.

"Mother," I said, my voice low. I stepped in front of her, so she couldn't help but stop moving. "What did you do?" I repeated, this time slower. I wasn't going anywhere until she told me.

"I had them fill out a questionnaire." She covered her face with her hands. "It's shameful, I know, but I needed to know where they stood in terms of holiday cheer."

"You what?"

Mom peeked at me through a slit in her fingers. "It was done in good faith, I promise. I just had to know if I needed to amp up the Christmas spirit or if they would be happy just being here."

This was ridiculous. "And?"

Mom took in a deep breath. "Emilia is a Cindy Lou, but Beatrice..."

My ears perked at her name. Beatrice was cute and funny. Plus, she seemed more levelheaded than her friend. Em kept giggling at everything and looked more starry-eyed than most people who came to Christmasland.

"What about her?" I asked, trying to sound like I was hoping Mom would finish her sentence and not that I genuinely wanted to know.

Mom blew out her breath, causing her lips to vibrate. "She's a Grinch."

I snorted. The way Mom described these people was ridiculous. "You mean she's not obsessed with the Christmas spirit like you are?"

Mom shook her head as if the mere thought of someone like that was unfathomable. "I just don't understand how anyone could feel that way." She tapped her chin as if she were accessing her ideas on the rolodex in her mind.

I wanted to point out that her own son felt that way, but Mom would just respond by adding *more* decorations to my room, as if that were all it would take to cause my heart to grow. After stepping on a few nutcrackers and waking up to a creepy elf doll staring down at me, I realized that I needed to keep my lips sealed about my feelings toward Christmas while I stayed here.

Suddenly, her smile brightened, and she turned her focus on me. The look in her eyes was crazed, and I knew right away, I wanted no part in what she was about to say.

"I have an idea—"

"No." I emphasized my refusal with a quick shake of my head. "No, no, no."

Mom frowned. "I didn't even say anything."

"Doesn't matter. I can tell from the look in your eye that I want no part of this." I finished off the water, crumpled the bottle, and tossed it into the recycling. I moved to head outside, but Mom intercepted me.

"Why not? Why won't you help your poor mom out?" Her bottom lip quivered as she glanced up at me. It was effective, I'll give her that. But there was no way I wanted to trick two perfectly nice girls.

"It wouldn't be fair."

"But they're here for an experience," she said as she reached out and stopped me from opening the door. "It's only a few nights. Why not give them a magical experience that they will talk about for years to come?" She gave me a hopeful smile. "Every girl wants the perfect Hallmark experience, and we can give them that."

I studied her. If I hadn't experienced Emilia's excitement over the room just minutes ago, I would have called Mom crazy. But from the squeals and pure adoration that came from Emilia, I had to admit, Mom might be right.

Plus, what harm could come from it? After all, these people voluntarily came to a place called Christmasland and are staying at a place called the North Pole. It wasn't like they didn't walk into this world with open eyes. Who was I to stop them from experiencing a cheesy holiday show?

"Fine," I said as I slipped on my jacket. "Just keep me out of it."

Mom narrowed her eyes. "But you're the perfect character."

"What?"

Mom waved her hand in front of me. "The Grinch-like hero who has come home from the big city. You're like every girl's dream."

That was not a term I'd ever heard someone use to describe me, and I wasn't sure how I felt about it coming from my mother. "What?" I asked again. Maybe my hearing was going. There was no way she was saying these words to me.

"You are the hero in every Hallmark movie." She grabbed my

arm and shook it a bit. "You are the perfect person to play the male lead."

I'd had enough. There was no way I was going to stand here and listen to this. "I'm going out to get firewood for the rooms." I let out a whistle, and Rudolph rose from his bed. He waddled over to me, and I pulled open the door to let him out.

"I really need your help," she said as she moved to let me pass.

I paused right before I stepped outside. Then I shook my head and gave her a small smile. "I can't. Find someone else."

Fifteen minutes later, a car pulled into the driveway of the inn and parked in the back. I was in the middle of swinging the axe, so I waited until I split the log in half before I looked up. Porter opened the door and stepped out. He was dressed in a suit and tie. Not something I normally saw from my out-of-work cousin.

"Hey," I called out as I set the axe by the wood-chopping stump and headed over to intercept him.

Porter looked on edge. His gaze ran up and down me as he waited for me to join him.

"Hey," he said with an awkward head nod.

I studied him. "What are you doing here, and why are you dressed like that?" I motioned toward his suit.

Porter cleared his throat as he adjusted his tie. "Aunt Carol said she had a job for me."

"A job?"

Porter nodded. "An acting job. Apparently, she wants me to play some rich out-of-towner?"

Oh no.

"She what?"

Porter looked startled by my sudden outburst. "She said she had a job for me. I am, as you know, a trained actor. She wants me to play the part of a rich businessman from New York." His expression turned serious as he met my gaze. He looked as if he were challenging me.

"Did she say for whom she wanted you to play the part?"

Porter paused and squinted as if he were trying to recall. "I think she said some out-of-town girls." He hesitated and then shrugged. "I don't know. She said, 'paying job,' and I came."

I parted my lips, but Porter didn't wait for me to respond. Instead, he clapped me on the shoulder and gave me a quick nod. "I'll see you inside."

My brain scrambled to say something, but he was gone before the shock wore off. This was taking things to a whole new level.

I needed to talk to Mom, and I needed to talk to her now. It wasn't nice to manipulate these girls like this. After all, I knew what it was like to be lied to. To be used. The woman who'd done that took my heart and ripped it from my chest.

I wasn't sure Beatrice and Emilia would have a similar reaction if they learned that their experiences here had been fabricated. They might even laugh about it and thank my mother for giving them an authentic holiday experience.

But that wasn't a risk I was willing to take. Beneath the surface, there was always a desire for things to be real. Even though I knew Scarlet wasn't the one for me, that didn't change my hope that she might be the woman I was meant to spend my life with.

When that hope was taken away from me, I was left with a hemorrhaging heart and a broken self-esteem. It was not an experience anyone should have to go through.

So, Mom may be determined to fabricate happiness for these two girls, but I wasn't going to have any part of it.

Nothing she said would change my mind. I was here to work, and that was it. I'd leave the acting up to everyone else.

I wasn't going to play this game of hers.

I would stand firm.

6

BEATRICE

Christmasland

E m and I unpacked our clothes into the ornate, dark wood dressers that we found in the large, walk-in closet. Once we were done, Em cuddled up on the couch and began scrolling through the channels on the TV in search of a Christmas movie while I looked over the calendar of events that I found on the desk.

"There's a snowball fight tonight," I said to no one in particular. I raised my eyebrows as I looked at the pictures of previous snowball fights. "It looks intense."

"Mm-hmm," Em said as she settled on a Hallmark movie. A man and a woman were speaking to each other. Apparently, there was some big misunderstanding between them.

Typical.

"Ooo, Santa will be in town on Saturday," I said as I scanned down the paper. "I wonder if he'll be surprised that we're in his room." I laughed at my own joke, but Em didn't seem as if she were paying attention.

I read the rest of the events in my mind. Lots of couple activities. I wondered for a moment what it would be like to come here with someone other than my best friend. Someone who was a man. Who loved me.

The idea of a sleigh ride and roasting marshmallows by a campfire seemed like the perfect way to spend the holidays if I were completely honest. But then I sighed. That was never going to happen. After my last boyfriend, Dirk, I'd sworn off men. They did nothing but break your heart.

"Are you okay?"

Em's voice and sudden appearance startled me. I yelped and threw the paper as if it had burned me.

Her eyebrows rose as she bent down to pick it up. "What were you looking at?" she asked with implication in her tone.

I sighed as I brought my feet up onto the chair and rested my chin on my knees. The last thing I needed for my sanity was to think about Dirk.

"It's just the calendar," Em said as she set the paper down on the desk. "Why did you act like it was something untoward?"

I tipped my head forward and rested my forehead on my knees. I took in a deep breath. "I was thinking about Dirk," I whispered.

"Why? Why were you thinking about that loser?" She bent down so that she was level with me. "We are here to have fun, not to think about men who are puny and jerks."

I lifted my head and met her gaze. I knew she was talking sense, but whenever I opened the locked door that was Dirk, it was hard to close it again. I laid my head back down and sighed. "I know," I whispered.

We sat there in silence for a few moments before Em reached over and patted my hand. "Let's go see what's going on in the North Pole."

I closed my eyes. I wanted to say no and spend the night holed up in this room, but I didn't want to leave Em to her own devices. She would come back having signed me up to be Mary in the

Nativity play. If I wanted a low-key vacation, I was going to need to keep tabs on her.

I refreshed my makeup along with Em. Fifteen minutes later, we had our shoes on and were standing in the hallway while Em locked our door. Soft Christmas music could be heard from downstairs, and it grew louder as we made our way to the first floor.

We stood at the bottom of the stairs and looked around. A man was playing the piano in the living room and he was accompanied by the sound of crackling fire. It really was a picturesque image.

"Did you get settled in?" Carol asked.

We turned to see her pass by us with a plate of cookies. She set them on the buffet in the dining room across from the living room. Everything smelled like a mixture of vanilla and cinnamon down here as well. It made me wonder if she pumped it through the ventilation system or something.

"We did. It's beautiful up there," Em said as she followed her.

Carol turned around and gave Em a wide grin. She seemed so incredibly happy that it was strange to me. After all, she literally lived Christmas every day. Didn't she ever get tired of it?

A wet sensation brushed my fingers. I yelped and jumped. When I glanced down, Rudolph looked up at me with his big brown eyes. His coat was dusted with snow, and behind him, Ethan was walking through the open door. His boots clomped on the floor as he shook out his hair. Wood was stacked in his arms, so he kicked the front door closed behind him.

"Make sure all of the rooms are stocked," Carol shouted as he slipped off his boots and headed up the stairs.

"That's your son?" Em asked.

I wanted to shush her. There was no need to fuel the fire that I knew was raging inside of her. The last thing I needed was for her to come up with another reason why everything was part of a bigger, overarching plot to give us the perfect Hallmark experience.

"Yes. I have three. He's the only one that has come home for the holiday." Carol was adjusting the plates of hors d'oeuvres on the buffet. "He's a lawyer in Chicago, but he needed a change of pace." Carol leaned in toward us. "That's what happens when you date your boss."

"You don't say," Em said as she flicked her gaze over to me and her smile widened.

I just shook my head. She was crazy.

"What are the festivities for the night?" I asked, needing to change the subject.

Carol's eyes glistened as she clapped her hands. "Dinner is in about an hour. We've got ham and cheesy potatoes on the menu. Then we have a cookie bake-off. Then there is a snowball fight in town." She waggled her finger in my direction. "Lots of things to do."

"Sounds amazing," Em breathed. She looked like she'd died and gone to heaven.

"You have to explore the town," Carol said. "In fact, Ethan should take you out; I know your car is still in the shop. I'm sure once he's done, he'd love to take you to explore."

I wanted to say that I doubted her assumption of his enthusiasm, but she didn't give me a chance. Instead, she patted our arms as she passed by us to head upstairs after Ethan. I watched her leave and then turned to face Em.

"We can't possibly ask him to take us into town." I attempted to hide my desperation, but I was failing miserably. When Em didn't answer, I turned to see her looking intently into the living room. I followed her gaze and discovered that a very well-dressed man was sitting on the couch with a newspaper in his hands.

"Em," I said as I shook her shoulder.

She startled and whipped her gaze over to me. "What?"

"You're staring."

Her cheeks flushed as she dropped her gaze down to her clasped hands. "I am, aren't I." She peered over at the man for a moment before she focused back on me. "I was just wondering if maybe he—"

"Em, no. Don't."

Her expression turned innocent. "I don't know what you are talking about."

I needed to put to rest her assumption that every person, every experience was all part of a plan to give her the perfect Christmas. "He's probably here to vacation as well."

She gave me a no-nonsense look. "By himself?"

I glanced over at him. "You don't know he's alone."

"Then I'll ask."

Carol was descending the stairs. She looked flustered, but as soon as she saw us, her smile returned. "Good news," she exclaimed. "Ethan said he'd love to take you out."

I highly doubted he'd used the word *love*.

"Carol, can I ask you a question?" Em pulled Carol further into the dining room.

"Sure, darling."

Em leaned close. "Who is that man?"

Carol followed her nod with her gaze, and when it landed on the man in the living room, she smiled. "That's Porter. He's visiting from New York just like you two. Apparently, he's from some mogul family there. Maybe you've heard of them." She tapped her chin. "McSally?"

I shook my head. There were literally thousands of rich families in New York. And there were none that lived in my part of town. Em elbowed me, and I turned to give her a dirty look. I was beginning to realize that it was her way of saying, *See? I told you so.*

"Is he alone?" Em asked. I could see her intrigue growing with every word.

Carol nodded. "He's here by himself." Then her expression

morphed to one of excitement. "Do you want me to introduce you two?"

Em nodded. "Definitely."

"Wait." I reached out and grabbed Em's arm. "What about going into town?"

She wiggled from my grasp. "You go with Ethan. After all, you need the full Christmas experience." She gave me one last smile as she hurried after Carol, who had crossed the foyer and was heading toward Porter.

Now alone, I sighed. I'd been ditched by my best friend. Great.

I reached out and grabbed a cookie. I was only halfway through it when I heard Ethan coming down the stairs. He was back to wearing his tan jacket and looked perturbed. His gaze landed on me, and his scowl deepened.

Man, he had the Scrooge bit down to an art.

"Ready?" he asked as he crossed the foyer and slipped on his boots. This time, he laced them up.

I wanted to skip out. With Em distracted, I just might be able to slip upstairs for some much-needed silence, but there was no way I wanted to tell the grinch in front of me that I didn't need him to take me anywhere.

"Yep," I said as I moved to grab my jacket.

"Ethan." Carol's voice startled me. I turned to see that she was standing the foyer, Em-less. I could only imagine what was going on in the other room. I was certain that I was a distant memory to my friend.

"Help her with her jacket," Carol said as she waved in my direction.

"I'm good," I said, but Carol didn't seem to notice me. She and Ethan were engaging in an epic stare-down.

It ended with Ethan sighing, reaching over to grab a light-pink jacket, and shaking it out. Carol looked satisfied with his reaction as she disappeared into the dining room. I turned to see Ethan standing there with the jacket open and ready for me to slip my arms into it.

Ethan look so agitated that I almost didn't want to tell him that it wasn't my jacket, but I also didn't want to go gallivanting around town in a coat that wasn't mine.

"That one is mine," I said as I motioned to the dark-grey jacket on the hook.

Ethan looked down at the jacket and then up to mine. He sighed as he returned the pink coat to the hook and grabbed my grey one. He shook it out and held it up.

I slipped my arms into it as he pulled the jacket up onto my shoulders. It was strange, standing this close to a man. It had been a while. I felt tiny in comparison to Ethan's six-foot frame. He towered over me, and when he was standing this close, it was as if I could feel his warmth even though he wasn't touching me.

It was a strange sensation, and I wasn't sure how I felt about it. My first reaction was to step away, but there was a part of me—a small part—that didn't want to move. And that scared me.

"Ready?" Ethan asked. His tone had softened, and it sent shivers down my spine. It was almost as if he realized that he had been short with me and felt bad about it.

"Yes," I said as I nodded and turned toward the door.

He turned the handle and pulled it open. I walked out onto the deck, with Ethan closely following behind me. He stayed close as we descended the porch steps and headed over to his car. He'd parked toward the back of the house, and our feet crunched on the snow as we walked toward it.

When we got there, he opened the passenger door and waited for me to get in. After I slipped onto the seat, he shut the door and hurried to the other side.

The sun was setting behind the trees, and the lights around the inn were starting to flicker on. The windows were illuminated, and it gave me a strangely warm feeling as I studied the house.

Ethan pulled out of the driveway, and I couldn't keep myself from staring at the scene in front of me. It really was beautiful.

I sighed. I hated to say it, but Em had been right. Coming here had soothed my soul in a way that I hadn't realized I needed.

"Everything okay?" Ethan asked once we were on the road and headed into town.

I glanced over at him. He was staring at the road as he drove. I wasn't sure if he was just being nice or if he was actually interested in what I had to say. Hoping it was the latter, I shrugged.

"I guess I didn't realize how calming it would be to stay in a house decked out in holiday cheer." I settled back in my seat and watched as the decorated houses passed us by.

Ethan chuckled. "Yeah, I always forget that. It's been a while since I've been here."

His response startled me. I didn't peg him as the talkative type. He seemed deep and brooding. To have him open up like this was…strange.

"If you have a place like this to go to every year, why have you stayed away?"

Ethan glanced over at me. His gaze roamed my face for a moment before he turned his attention back to the road. "I needed a break. Mom is great, but she can be intense."

A soft smile played on my lips. "I like her."

"Mom?"

I nodded.

Ethan turned down Main Street, and the entire town was ablaze with twinkling Christmas lights. "This town does not disappoint." I breathed out as I peered out the window.

Ethan laughed. "Oh, you'd be surprised. This is just the beginning."

7

ETHAN

T he further I drove into town, the deeper my regret became. I shouldn't have let Mom threaten me into taking Beatrice out anywhere. But when she came barreling into the room that I was stocking with firewood and declared it was my responsibility as her son to help her out, I agreed just to get her off my back.

After all, if I didn't do it now, Mom was going to hound me for the rest of my stay. And that cut into my ability to hide away from the world and lick my emotional wounds.

Plus, Beatrice seemed nice enough. She wasn't as crazy as her friend. It appeared that she had a sensible head on her shoulders. And that's what I needed. People who came to Christmasland were crazy. They loved everything about the holiday season, and it was hard to have a conversation with the tourists that didn't end up being about cookies or tinsel.

I doubted our conversation was going to be like that at all.

"This is incredible," Beatrice said as she peered out her window. All the shops were brightly lit from either the Christmas lights hung on every ledge or the large window displays that depicted holiday cheer.

Having been here for a few weeks, I was starting to get used to seeing this on a daily basis. I had lost the shock and awe that every newcomer experiences. In a way, watching a calm look cross Beatrice's face made me jealous. I wanted to feel that way again about this place.

I guess you should never see how something is made. It ruins the illusion. Despite what visitors thought, Christmasland was like any other small town—once you took out their obsession with Christmas. People lived. People died. Mortgages were paid, and debt was accrued.

But visitors didn't see that. Instead, they saw a place that gave them what they expected the holidays to be. Happy, stress-free, and covered in cinnamon-scented pinecones.

I saw an empty parking space next to the sidewalk and pulled into it. I let the engine idle for a moment as I glanced over at Beatrice. She didn't look worried as she moved to unbuckle her seatbelt.

Needing to put together a game plan in my head, I reached out my hand to stop her from leaving, but then I realized that I was close to touching this stranger and pulled my hand back. "What exactly do you want to do while we're here?"

Beatrice glanced over at me. "I'm not sure. I guess, I've never been to a place like this." She furrowed her brow. "What do you suggest?"

"Do you want the Christmasland special or the Ethan special?" As soon as those words left my lips, I felt like an idiot. There was no way she wanted to experience the Ethan special. After all, it was just the spots that helped me maintain my sanity while I lived in a snow globe.

Beatrice looked as if she were fighting a smile. "What's the Ethan special?"

I shook my head. "You have to decide before I tell you."

She paused and then nodded. "You have me intrigued. As long

as it's not taking me into the middle of the forest and leaving me to die, I'm going to go with the Ethan special."

For some insane reason, my heart rate picked up from her choice. I knew I shouldn't read into it, but I couldn't help it. It made me feel good.

I opened the door. "All right. Let's do it, then."

She waited for me as I rounded the car, and we started walking down the sidewalk together. We had to dodge a few large groups who were oohing and aahing over the window displays of Christmasland Bank. Each section depicted a different scene from *A Christmas Story*.

Beatrice laughed and pointed to the leg lamp. I just nodded as I watched her. She didn't seem as crazy about Christmas as Emilia was, but I could see the magic working inside of her.

"So why aren't you with your family this year?" I asked after we passed by the bank and were making our way down the street. I had my hands tucked into my jacket pockets, and Beatrice was tightening her scarf around her neck.

"I don't have much of a family," she said. Her tone was soft but matter-of-fact.

I glanced over at her. "You don't have a family?"

She smiled. The sun was gone now, and the wind had picked up, swirling her hair around. Her cheeks were pink, and every so often, I could see that so were the tips of her ears.

"I'm a foster kid. My parents left me at a fire station when I was just a baby." She chuckled. "It sounds straight out of a movie, but it is what it is."

"I'm so sorry," I said, feeling like a jerk for bringing it up.

She shook her head. "No need. I struggled with it when I was growing up, but now..." She paused in front of Sugarplum Bakery and peered in at the delectable goodies that were displayed in the window. "Now I'm okay," she whispered. I wondered for a moment if she believed those words or was just saying them for my benefit.

"Can we get some of those?" She turned to me as she pointed toward the cinnamon sugar–covered doughnut twists. "Or is this not part of the Ethan special."

"Doughnuts are always part of the Ethan special." I pulled the door open and waited for Beatrice to walk through. Once inside, the smell of sugar and fried dough assaulted me. I took in a deep breath at the same time Beatrice did.

It was as if we both had to stop moving just to breathe. I glanced down at her, and she was grinning up at me. "I think this is what heaven is like," she said as she moved over to the large glass displays that lined the walls. "How are people who live here not three hundred pounds?" She grabbed a bag and a wax sheet and started inspecting what was available.

"Hey, Ethan," Shelly, the bakery owner, said as she came up from behind me. I turned to see her too wide smile aimed my direction. She was a few years younger than me, and I couldn't help but think she was trying to start something.

And Mom didn't help matters. She'd been asking me to take Shelly out on a date every day since I got here. It was annoying, to say the least.

"Shelly," I said as I nodded toward her.

Beatrice had straightened, and a curious look crossed her face. Her gaze was flicking between Shelly and me.

"Hi, I'm Shelly." She reached her hand out to Beatrice. "I own the bakery."

"Bea," Beatrice said as she shook Shelly's hand. There was an awkward pause, but then they both dropped each other's hand. Beatrice glanced around. "This is an amazing place. I can't wait to try some of these." She tipped her head toward the doughnuts.

"Thanks. It's what I love."

I tried not to notice, but I could have sworn Shelly moved closer to me as she spoke. When her arm brushed mine, I realized that I had been right. She was practically linking arms with me.

I glanced down at the nonexistent space between us and took

a step to the left to get away from her. I was fairly certain what she was trying to do, and it was ridiculous. I wasn't hers, and I wasn't Beatrice's. I had no intention of dating anyone right now.

I was perfectly fine being single.

"I can imagine," Beatrice said. Her tone was low and almost reverent. It made me wonder what her reaction was about. Did she not do what she loved?

"Do you bake?" Shelly asked.

Beatrice snorted. "Not really."

"Oh, I'm sure you're not that bad."

Beatrice stopped as she studied Shelly. "I never said I was bad. I just don't bake on the regular."

Shelly's fake smile deepened. She reached out and swatted at Beatrice's arm. "Oh, I'm sorry. That's what people normally mean when they say they don't bake." Then she glanced up at me and giggled.

Not sure what was going on, I kept my reaction stoic as I folded my arms across my chest. I definitely was not on Shelly's side if that was what she was asking me to do.

"Oh, I have the greatest idea. Tomorrow, we are having a bake-off here. You should come. I'd love to taste some of your baked goods." Her eyebrows were so high, they almost disappeared into her hairline. I wasn't sure if she thought the expression would convince Beatrice, but it was scaring me.

"I, um…" Beatrice glanced around, and then a determined look crossed her face. "I'll be there."

Shelly clapped her hands. "Perfect." Then she turned to me. "I forgot to tell you, but your mom signed you up to be a judge." She patted my arm.

"She what?" I started, but someone called Shelly's name and she nodded and headed in their direction.

Now alone with Beatrice, I blinked a few times. How had this turned from something between Shelly and Beatrice, to a commitment between Shelly and me? My lips were parted as I focused my attention back on Beatrice, who looked as perturbed as I felt.

"Idiot," she whispered under her breath as she turned back to the display cases and started shoving doughnuts into the bag.

"Me?" I asked as I moved to stand next to her.

Her cheeks flushed as she hurriedly glanced up at me. "Oh, no. Not you." She waved toward herself with the tongs. "Yours truly."

"Why are you an idiot? You aren't stuck with judging a bake-off."

She snorted. "That's the easy part. I"—she took in a deep breath—"can't bake." She lowered her voice as she glanced around as if to make sure no one was listening. "Like, I set off fire alarms when I try."

A chuckle escaped as I took in her alarmed expression. She looked terrified.

I leaned forward. I couldn't help it. Beatrice was adorable. "I'm sure you're not that bad," I whispered.

When I pulled back, I suddenly realized that I'd been only inches from her face. Out of pure ridiculous instinct, my gaze flicked down to her lips. Heat pricked my skin as I straightened and cleared my throat. There was something wrong with me. I wasn't the kind of guy who flirted. And I certainly wasn't the kind of guy who entertained relationships with anyone who voluntarily came to Christmasland.

Beatrice's cheeks had flushed a deeper pink, and I wondered if it was because she enjoyed how close I got or hated it. Her gaze didn't help answer that question either. She looked just as confused as I felt.

Wanting to move the conversation away from the deep waters we'd just waded into, I moved toward the cash register and took out my wallet. "Four doughnuts," I told Shelly's sister who was standing behind the counter.

She rang me up despite Beatrice's insistence that she could pay for it.

The truth was, I didn't want to wait around while Beatrice fished out her money. I was ready to get out of this bakery and out into the open air. I didn't like the desire that was brewing inside of my stomach or the fact that, for a moment, I'd forgotten about Scarlet and what she'd done to me.

For a moment, the happiness I felt had overshadowed the pain that I'd been convinced was a permanent feature in my soul.

And that thought scared me. If I wasn't hurting, who was I? If I wasn't hurting, I was going to have the face the reality of why Scarlet treated me the way she did.

I was going to have to come to terms with the fact that I was just unlovable.

That wasn't a realization that I wanted to have here, in Sugarplum Bakery, surrounded by Christmas music and holiday-themed baked goods.

This was not where I wanted to reach my lowest of lows.

If that happened, I was fairly certain I wasn't going to come back from it.

Ever.

8

BEATRICE

E than was quiet as we walked out of the bakery and back out onto the sidewalk. I held tightly to the bag of doughnuts as I quickened my pace behind him. I wasn't sure what had happened in there, but whatever it was had taken us from laughing to silent in an instant.

And I couldn't help but wonder if I'd done something to spur this change.

Sure it had been stupid to agree to the baking contest. I wasn't sure what I was thinking, but as soon as I saw the smug smile on Shelly, I lost all ability to think rationally. It was as if she were laughing at me, and the only thing I could do was declare that I *could* bake, thus accepting her invitation.

I stood by my previous assessment—I was an idiot.

"Everything okay?" I asked as I hurried to fall in step with Ethan.

He glanced down at me for a moment before he slowed his pace and sighed. "Yeah. I'm fine."

We were at a comfortable stroll now, and his relaxed demeanor made me feel better.

"Oh, good. I was worried there for a second that I'd done something wrong."

He chuckled. "No. You didn't do anything."

"So you're not upset that I agreed to the competition? I mean, I know my baking is bad, but I didn't know the news had made its way to Christmasland." I smiled at my dumb joke, but Ethan just looked confused. I hurried to add, "It's legendary how bad my baking skills are..."

He still looked confused.

I shook my head. "Never mind."

Ethan paused. We must have made our way into a quieter part of town. This looked like the business district. Most of the buildings were dark, and there were only a few people mulling around. It was such a strange contrast from where we had just been. It made me realize Christmasland was just like any other town. There was the tourist area and then there was the place that the everyday residents saw.

It was kind of a relief to see some normalcy. Not everything here had to be decked out in Christmas lights.

"Is this the part of the story where you kill me?" I asked.

Ethan chuckled and shook his head. "If it was, do you think I would tell you?"

"Touché," I said.

Ethan made his way over to a small convenience store and pulled open the door. "This is the true gem of Christmasland."

I furrowed my brow as I headed into the tiny store. The shelves were packed full of all sorts of food. Some of the labels I couldn't read. I glanced over at Ethan. He looked right at home as he picked up a few bags of snacks and then made his way to the small man at the register.

"Hey, Anders," he said as he set the food down on the counter.

"How's it going, Ethan?" Anders asked. His accent was thick, and I was trying to figure out where it was from. "Enjoying your evening?"

Ethan nodded, and warmth filled my chest. Was it because he was spending time with me? Or that he'd finally escaped the North Pole? Either way, he said he was enjoying our time together. I was going to pat myself on the back for that one.

"A coffee as well?" Anders asked as he rang up the items.

Ethan held up two fingers. "Two actually." Then he paused. "You drink coffee, right?"

I nodded, and Ethan turned his attention back to Anders. "Two."

After they rang up the items, Ethan hung the bag on his wrist and grabbed the coffees. He looked more at ease here than I'd ever seen him. Which wasn't saying a lot since I'd just met the guy. Still, I felt like I could say with some authority, Ethan was in his element.

"Come on," he said as he pushed open the back door and nodded toward some stairs that went up.

I furrowed my brow as I glanced over at Anders. He didn't seem alarmed that Ethan had opened what looked like a restricted door. In fact, Anders had settled down on the seat behind the counter and was busy reading the newspaper.

Realizing that we weren't going to be reprimanded, I nodded and followed after Ethan. The door slammed shut behind us as we started our ascension. Seeing Anders reading the newspaper sparked a question inside of me. Realizing we might have some time before we got to wherever Ethan was taking us, I glanced behind me.

"What does the town newspaper report on?"

Ethan's gaze met mine. "Probably what's going on around town."

"Well, of course. But what does Christmasland's newspaper report on? Missing cookies? Sleigh marks on the roof? Reindeer going awry?" I giggled at the atrocities that a town with this much cheer could have.

"Some of the reports are like that."

I dropped my jaw. "I was joking."

Ethan shrugged. "This is Christmasland. Wouldn't it be strange if they didn't have stories like that?"

I nodded. "True."

Ethan sighed. "In reality, Christmasland is just like any other town. There are legal fights over boundaries. People wanting to build things on public property. Taxes. All sorts of stuff."

I wrinkled my nose. We were at the top landing, and the only other place for us to go was through the metal door to our left. I waited for Ethan to lead the way.

"That's kind of disappointing," I said as he walked past me.

He paused and glanced down. "That we pay taxes?"

I shook my head. "Not that. I guess…with all the things going on in the world, wouldn't it be nice if Christmasland was exactly that? Just a place where every happy Christmas event could take place without the mundane aspects of life?" I was starting to understand the whimsy of this place. The desire to step away from your current problems and hide where everything seemed perfect.

Like every holiday movie.

"Is that what you really want?"

I hadn't noticed Ethan studying me. He was still standing there, staring down at me. I blinked as I tried to step back but was met by the stair railing. The intensity of his stare made my cheeks flush, and all I could do was shrug.

"Isn't that what everyone wants?"

He held my gaze for a moment longer before he sighed and shifted the coffees to one arm while he used his free hand to open the door. A blast of cold air surrounded us.

The stairs had brought us to the top of the building, and as we stepped out onto the snow-covered roof, I sucked in my breath. Partly because the wind was making it hard to breathe, but the other part was from the scene that played out in front of me. We were up high enough that we could see everything.

The trees all lit up. The lights strung from the lamp posts. The warm yellow glow of the shop windows. In the middle of it all was a gigantic tree that rose up above the surrounding small shops.

"This is beautiful," I whispered. But I wasn't sure if Ethan heard me. The wind whipped around my face and carried my words off with it.

"It is."

I startled and turned to see Ethan standing right next to me. He handed over one of the coffees, and I gratefully took it. I wrapped my hands around the cardboard cup and allowed the heat to warm my fingers.

"I'm sorry, I normally just get a coffee with sugar." He winced. "Do you take cream?"

"This is good." The memory of the mint creamer from the coffee shop with Em came flooding back to me. "I've been betrayed by creamers before."

Ethan looked confused.

"Why do they have to make everything holiday themed? Who wants to put mint in their coffee? It's like drinking toothpaste." I shuddered at the thought.

"Wait. You hate holiday creamer, too?" He looked so shocked that it made me laugh.

"Yes. Pumpkin spice? What even is that?"

He nodded more fervently this time. And then he smiled. A genuine smile. It was as if the clouds parted on his face and the sun shone through. I couldn't pull my gaze away.

He was good-looking, just like the brooding hero of any story. But with that smile—it put him on a completely different level.

Then I felt like an idiot. Curse Em and her ridiculous ideas. I was beginning to adopt them and sound crazy in my own mind. Sure, I was a writer, so it wasn't too strange for me to classify Ethan as a hero, but that didn't mean he was *my* hero. I needed to get that straight.

So I turned and focused my attention back on the lights of the town. "So is this your special hideout spot?" I asked between sips of coffee. The hot liquid helped warm my body.

"Yeah. You should feel special that I shared it with you." He opened up one of the bags he'd bought and tipped it toward me.

"Funyuns?" I asked as I took one out.

"The best kind of chip."

I took a bite and shrugged. "That's debatable."

We munched on the food in silence. Once my coffee was gone and I was fairly certain I had no more feeling in my toes, I shoved my hands into the pockets of my jacket and turned to face Ethan. "Skip the forest, all you need to do is bring me up here, and I'll freeze to death."

Ethan glanced over at me, and his smile turned to concern. "Are you cold? You're cold. Let's get you down from here."

I chuckled as he hurriedly gathered everything and then waved me toward the door. Once we were downstairs, he tossed our empty coffee cups and called a goodbye to Anders as he pushed open the door. When we got back to his car, I climbed inside as he started the engine, making sure to start the seat warmers as well.

We made our way back to the festive part of town. As we drove by, he waved toward the stores. "Do you still want to go in some?"

My nose was frozen, and my fingertips were prickling as they started warming up. "I'm good. Em and I can come here tomorrow." The thought of a warm fire filled my mind, and suddenly, that was all I wanted. "Plus, your mom's ham and potatoes sound amazing."

Ethan chuckled as he pulled past the shops and kept going down the street toward the North Pole. By the time we got back to the bed and breakfast, I was officially warmed. Ethan parked in the back, and as he pulled his keys out of the ignition, he reached his hand out to stop me.

"I'll get your door," he said.

Before I could respond, he was unbuckled and jogging around the hood of the car. When he got to my door, he pulled it open and stood there, waiting for me to get out.

He looked more relaxed than he had early in the evening. It was strange that he wanted to act gentlemanly towards me. After all, he'd seemed to fight his mom when she told him to get my coat, yet now he was voluntarily offering to assist me.

I didn't want to read into it, but I couldn't help the butterflies in my stomach starting to wake up. Did he want to be around me? Was I crazy enough to hope?

We walked side by side toward the inn. We rounded the house and climbed the front porch steps. He opened the door, and I made my way into the foyer. Laughter came from the dining room, and when I peeked inside, I saw that most of the guests were either gathered around the table or off sitting on one of the plush chairs in the corner. The salty smell of ham mixed with the warmth of the fire made me feel...at home.

Two hands gripped the collar of my jacket, and a moment later, Ethan helped me slip it off and hung it on the coat rack behind me. My skin tingled at his touch, and even after he took his jacket off and headed into the dining room, my entire body felt on fire.

It could be that I was still warming up from standing outside, but deep down, I doubted that. In fact, I was beginning to fear the real reason why I was responding like this toward Ethan.

I kind of liked him.

Which I didn't want to do. Not here. Not now. It was ridiculous.

I spotted Em and walked straight over to her. Carol called out that she'd fix me a plate, and I waved my thanks but kept my focus on Em. She was sitting next to Porter on the couch, giggling and swatting his arm.

I plopped down in the small space to her left, and that caused the two of them to scoot over, so I could have more room. "Did you miss me?" I asked.

Em glanced over at me. "Oh, were you gone?"

I gave her an annoyed look.

She laughed and patted my knee. "I'm just kidding. I know you were gone. Porter has been keeping me company, so I wouldn't miss you too much."

I tipped my head past Em and nodded at Porter. "Nice to meet you."

"Likewise."

I rested my head back and took in a deep breath. I didn't want to look around to locate Ethan, but I couldn't help it. I found him in the corner, eating a plate of food that I could only assume Carol brought him. He was back to brooding.

I dropped my gaze. I was an idiot to keep wondering what he was thinking. What he was doing.

"How did it go with Mr. Grinch?" Em asked me, drawing me out of my thoughts.

I glanced over at her. "It was fine."

Porter snorted. "Just fine?"

We both looked over at him. He looked surprised, and then a smile emerged. "I mean, I've only been here a few days, but from what I've seen, he's not the friendliest of guys."

"He's not?" Em asked.

I wanted to defend Ethan. After all, he seemed perfectly nice to me. It felt like he'd opened up to me when we were on the rooftop. But Porter had been around longer than me; perhaps what I saw was just an anomaly. Maybe Ethan was just playing a part with me.

"I'm tired," I said as I closed my eyes. But a moment later, Carol brought by a plate of food. The smell and my stress mixed together and made me ravenous. I ate and listened to Em and Porter talk about their favorite Christmas traditions.

Every so often, my gaze found its way back over to Ethan, but after an indulgence of a few seconds, I pulled my attention back to my food.

Nothing was going to happen between us. This wasn't some Hallmark movie where I melt the heart of the town's grinch. This was just a place where they decorated for Christmas, and it was up to the tourist to remember the truth.

I needed to stick to reality.

I was here for only a few more days, and then I would head back home. There was no need to get consumed by what I thought might happen instead of focusing on what was actually happening.

I was allowing myself to be attracted to a man I was never going to see again. That was foolish and needed to stop.

Right now.

9

ETHAN

I tried not to keep tabs on Beatrice throughout the night, but it was hard to keep from paying attention to what she was doing or where she was going. The curse of staying in the same house as the person you were trying to avoid. They ended up being everywhere.

It was fun to watch her during the Christmas cookie decorating contest. Mom had designated me the frosting filler, which meant I could move around the room, keeping an eye on what was going on without looking like a creeper.

Beatrice spent the time laughing and decorating with Emilia, and it was almost as if what she'd told me about not liking Christmas wasn't true. In fact, she looked perfectly at home spreading frosting on the cookies and sprinkling sugar crystals on top. It was hard to imagine that Christmas had not been a part of her past like it had been mine. And that caused me to start thinking about what she said to me while we were in town.

She'd grown up in the foster system, which meant she most likely didn't have the kind of Christmas celebrations I'd had growing up. She'd been disappointed when I joked about Christmasland being just like every other town out there. It was as if I'd told her that Santa didn't exist when she asked how he fit down the chimney.

That made me sad. Sad enough to start entertaining the proposition that Mom had presented to me earlier today. When she asked me to facilitate giving Beatrice the best Christmas experience ever.

Would there really be that much harm in participating?

Once the cookies were decorated, a group of guests decided that they were going to head into town for the snowball fight. I tried not to eavesdrop on Beatrice and Emilia's conversation. They were talking quietly as they stood by the doorway that led out to the foyer.

Emilia sounded as if she were begging Beatrice, who in turn was sighing and giving her friend an exasperated look.

"It'll be fun," Emilia said as she clung to Beatrice's arm.

Beatrice glanced down at her friend and then, for a moment, back up to me. Our gazes locked until I realized that she'd just discovered I was watching her. Out of sheer desperation to keep my thoughts to myself, I dropped my gaze and focused on clearing the table.

"I don't know, Em. I'm tired. A bath and then bed sounds amazing."

From the corner of my eye, I saw Emilia jut out her lip. "Please?"

Beatrice sighed. "Fine. One hour and then we're back here."

Emilia cheered as she rushed over to Porter to tell him the good news. I straightened and glanced over my shoulder at Beatrice. She stood there with her gaze downturned. I could tell she regretted what she'd said.

"It'll be fun," I offered before I could police my thoughts.

Beatrice glanced up at me. "It will?"

I'd already jumped in. I might as well keep going. "Yeah. It's pretty low-key. Families and couples and such. It's really just an excuse for George to sell more hot chocolate."

Beatrice smiled, and heat rushed over my skin. I couldn't help but smile back at her even though I was fairly certain my cheeks were bright red. Was it wrong that I enjoyed the fact that I could make her smile? Make her laugh? It felt like my own personal Christmas present to see her respond this way.

"George?" Then she narrowed her eyes. "How good is this hot chocolate?"

"Best in town. You can't miss his cart. He's normally around the gazebo in the center of town. His cart is called Santa's Milk."

Her smile softened as she studied me. My heart picked up speed as I tried to keep my reaction to myself. I wasn't sure how she felt about me, but my interest in her was starting to grow. Stronger than I cared to admit.

"Santa's Milk." She wrinkled her nose.

"I know. It's weird, but it's a fun cart. You'll enjoy it." I took a step forward and then regretted it when Beatrice straightened and glanced down at my feet. Had I made a mistake? I didn't want to make her uncomfortable.

"I'll keep an eye out for it."

"Bea," Emilia called from the front door, where she was waiting with Porter.

I tried to catch his gaze, but Porter wasn't complying. Instead, he just stood there looking pleased with himself.

"You driving them?" I asked. Everyone looked over at me, and I realized that I hadn't made an effort to police the bite to my tone. To everyone here, Porter was just another guest and I was the jerk yelling at him. "I'm sorry," I muttered.

"Yeah. Their car is still in the shop." Porter pushed his hand through his hair and gave me a *what was that for* look.

I wanted to respond. After all, he was my punk cousin, but Emilia looked so happy as she stood there, bouncing up and down on the balls of her feet and waving for Beatrice to hurry up.

Beatrice offered me a weak smile before she turned and

headed over to her friend. "I'll see you later?" she called over her shoulder as she lingered in the doorway.

My entire mood lightened as I realized she was waiting for me to respond. "Yeah. I'll be here," I said as I lifted the tray of discarded cookies.

Her smile broadened as she nodded. "Perfect."

She turned and walked out onto the porch, shutting the door behind her.

My gaze lingered on the door as I sighed. What was I doing? Why was I allowing myself to react this way? She was a guest, and I was hiding out here until my wounds healed enough for me to go back. I was an idiot to entertain thoughts like the ones I was currently suppressing.

I wasn't here to indulge in the idea of romance. I was here to work and forget. That was all.

I blew out my breath as I turned to focus on cleaning up the table. Just as I turned around, Mom's face popped into view. She was inches away, peering up at me with a smile that made me want to groan.

I moved to the other side of the table to continue cleaning only to have her follow after me. When it became apparent that she wasn't going to leave me alone, I clamped down on my frustration and turned to face her. "What's up?" I asked.

Mom folded her arms and narrowed her eyes. Her fingers tapped on her forearm as she studied me. "What happened in town? You didn't want to go, and then when you got back, you spent the entire evening staring at Beatrice."

"I did not spend the entire evening staring at anyone."

Mom nodded. "You're right. You spent the entire evening trying *not* to stare at Beatrice." Mom held still as her eyes darted back and forth.

"I did not do that," I lied as I moved to collect a few frosting bottles and place them on my tray.

"Mm-hmm," Mom said as she gathered a few empty cookie trays and followed me into the kitchen.

I placed my tray next to the sink and then turned to face her. "Hypothetically" —I narrowed my eyes— "hypothetically," I repeated, "if you wanted to give someone the perfect Christmas, how would you do that?"

Mom's eyebrows rose higher than I'd ever seen in my life. Her eyes widened, and I feared I'd made a huge mistake.

"Hypothetically," I whispered.

"Hypothetically," Mom responded, her voice breathy and full of relief.

I nodded.

Mom studied me for a moment before she turned on her heel and started walking over to her small office just off the kitchen. Not sure what she was doing, I followed but lingered next to the door instead of going inside.

A moment later, she emerged with a piece of paper in her hand. She waved it under my nose until I took it from her.

"Hallmark Bingo?" I glanced up at her.

She nodded.

"Holiday baking slash flour fight?" My gaze moved through the boxes. "Interrupted first kiss?" My body warmed at that one.

"Yes."

I glanced up to stare at her. "You want me to do these?"

She studied me before she shrugged. "If you want to give her the perfect Christmas experience, I can't think of anything more picturesque than a Hallmark movie. And if you don't want to watch them to understand, this is the next best thing." She tapped the paper with her forefinger.

As much as I wanted to call my mom crazy, she did have a point. Almost every woman I'd come across looked forward to the Hallmark Christmas movie-thon. And even though I hadn't originally pegged Beatrice for a watcher, she did seem to enjoy the cliché Christmas activities.

So what was the harm in creating moments just for her?

I folded up the paper and slipped it into my back pocket. "All right. I'll think about it," I said as I returned to the dining room to finish clearing the table.

When I brought the full tray back to the kitchen, Mom was elbow deep in soapy water. She was humming to herself as she washed the dishes. Christmas music played softly in the background, and she looked at peace.

I took a moment to study her. Mom had been so broken when Dad died. I worried that she was never going to crawl out of the hole she buried herself in. When she started focusing all of her attention on the house and Christmas, she started to become a spark of her old self.

I got my mother back.

Christmas gave her happiness that I was never going to understand. However, I was acutely aware of how healing the holiday could be. And I wanted that for Beatrice. I wanted her to experience Christmas to its fullest.

If it could heal my mother, I was certain it would have a good effect on Beatrice.

After the dining room was clean and the dishes were put away, I lingered in the living room with a book. The fire was dying down, so I stood and threw some logs on just as the front door opened and the sound of talking mixed with laughter filled the air.

I straightened and turned to see Beatrice standing in the doorway. She was smiling, her cheeks bright pink and her hair windblown. She was staring at someone I couldn't see as she slipped off her gloves and shoved them into her jacket pocket.

Before I could stop myself, I dusted off my hands and made my way toward her. It took her a second before she turned to face me. Her smile deepened.

"Have a good time?" I asked. I didn't make an attempt to hide my smile that appeared in response to hers.

She nodded. "It was fabulous. And Santa's Milk?" A dreamy expression passed over her face. "Incredible."

I laughed as I folded my arms and leaned against the doorjamb. "George knows what he is doing."

Emilia and Porter were taking off their jackets and hanging them up on the coat rack. As Beatrice removed hers, I stepped forward to take it from her. She hesitated as her gaze floated up to meet mine. There was a level of confusion in her eyes that had me regretting the move.

But I was already here, so I might as well keep going.

"I'll take that," I said as I shook off the snowflakes that were still clinging to it and moved past Emilia and Porter to hang it up.

"That's very gentlemanly," Emilia said. There was a hint of excitement to her voice that made me wince.

Was I that transparent?

"Yeah, thanks," Beatrice said. Her tone was quiet, as if I'd thrown her off.

"Well, I'm beat. I'm ready for a hot shower and bed." Emilia turned to face Porter. "I'll see you tomorrow morning for breakfast?"

I studied Porter to see what he was going to say. From what I knew, he didn't have a room here, and we were fully booked. I stifled a groan as he nodded. "Of course, I'll see you bright and early."

Emilia gave him a very wide and revealing smile before she locked arms with Beatrice and started dragging her to the stairs. Beatrice met my gaze one more time before she could no longer walk backwards and had to turn around.

Once they disappeared upstairs, I turned to face Porter, who was grinning. "Why are you smiling?"

Porter shrugged. "I haven't had a job in a long time. It feels good."

I winced at his words. To him, this was a job. I just hoped that Emilia wouldn't be crushed when she found out that my cousin was broke and not a millionaire looking for the small-town experience.

Not feeling as if I had any room to lecture him on authenticity, I folded my arms and stared him down. "Why did you say you were going to be here bright and early? We have no room in this inn."

"He's staying with you," Mom said as she walked up to us with a pile of folded towels in her arms. She handed them to Porter, who took them and offered me a wide smile.

Mom started to walk away just as my brain processed what she said. "He's what?" I asked as I followed after her.

She gave me an annoyed look. "Porter will be staying with you." She patted my shoulder. "Just like he did when you were kids and his family came to visit." She got a wistful look in her eyes. "Remember when you two insisted that you sleep in front of the Christmas tree, so you could see Santa?"

Porter laughed. "Oh right, that was hilarious when Uncle Steve dressed up and tried to surprise us."

Mom grew quiet at the mention of Dad's name. I peeked over at her to see that she was still smiling, just not as wide this time. "Yeah. Those were good times," she said, her voice barely a whisper.

Not wanting to argue with Mom while she was in this vulnerable state, I sighed and slapped Porter on the back. He flinched but didn't move to retaliate.

"I guess we can bunk up for old times' sake," I said as I squeezed his shoulder.

He winced but kept his forced smile. "It'll be fun."

Mom seemed satisfied and wandered off with Porter toward my room. I scrubbed my face and took in a deep breath. I was crazy. Crazy and stupid to think that this was remotely a good idea.

I couldn't help but wonder if there was going to come a point where I would regret the choices I made this evening. And a part of me said, yes, I was definitely going to regret them.

But then Beatrice's face floated into my mind, and suddenly, none of that mattered. Right now, all I wanted to do was give her a Christmas to remember.

I could survive the aftermath. As long as I was successful in that mission, I would be happy.

As long as Beatrice had a good time, I was willing to sacrifice whatever was necessary to make that a reality.

That was my Christmas mission, and I was ready to face it.

Head-on.

BEATRICE

Em was up bright and early the next day. She was hurrying around the room as if she had someplace she needed to be. When she slammed a dresser drawer for the fifth time that morning, I groaned and rolled to my side so I could see what she was doing.

Her back was to me, and I couldn't make out what had her in such a tizzy.

"Everything okay?" I asked as I stretched out on the bed. I allowed my body to sink into the plush mattress and fluffy pillows. The comforter was pulled up to my neck, and I buried myself deeper into the blanket.

If this was how I spent the next few days, I would be completely satisfied. I couldn't remember the last time I slept in like this, and I'd forgotten how heavenly it felt.

"We got an invitation to breakfast," Em said as she glanced over her shoulder. She was mid-swipe on her mascara, so her hand hovered just in front of her face.

"We what?" I sat up just in time to catch the envelope she flung in my direction. It was so lightweight that it only just made it to the edge of the mattress. I had to dive down to grab it before it disappeared under the bed.

Once I was situated again amongst the covers and pillows, I pulled out the folded-up piece of paper and smoothed it out.

We would love your presence this morning for the perfect Christmas breakfast. Please meet us downstairs at 8 a.m. sharp. Make sure to wear warm clothes.

Ethan and Porter

I started at the handwriting as I brushed the words with my fingertips. Had Ethan written this? Porter? It was strange that these two men got together to plan a breakfast, but maybe they'd become friends before we entered the picture. I made a mental note to ask Ethan about it when I saw him next.

And then my heart picked up speed. I was going to see Ethan again. The memories from the day before washed over me, and suddenly all I wanted to do was get ready, so I could verify why I felt this way.

I wanted to verify that, yes, Ethan was interested in me. At least, that was what I hoped.

"What aren't you telling me?"

I yelped and glanced up to see Em standing next to the bed, staring down at me. Her eyebrows were furrowed and her hands on her hips. I swallowed and shrugged as if I hadn't just been fantasizing about Ethan moments ago. "Nothing," I said as I pulled off the covers and dropped my feet to the dark-maroon plush carpet.

"What do you mean, nothing?" she asked, following behind me as I made my way to the bathroom. "I've never seen you smile like that before."

I paused before I shut the door. Then I turned. "Like what?"

A goofy smile spread across her face. She looked lovesick as she brought up her clasped hands to her face and batted her eyes. "Ethan," she said softly as she breathed out.

"I do not look like that," I said as I started shutting the door. Em stuck her foot into the bathroom, effectively stopping me.

"I'm not going anywhere. You're going to have to give me details about your trip into town with Ethan," she said as she slid her foot out and gave me a wicked smile.

I wanted to fight her but decided I would make better points when I was clean and dry. I started up the water, and once the steam had coated the room in a thick haze, I stepped in. I reveled in the shower of warm water as I sudsed up my hair. Once I was done, I wrapped one towel around my hair and another around my body and stepped out onto the plush bathmat. It was both warm and soft, and there was this calming sensation that spread through me as I stood on it.

It was strange to be so mesmerized by a simple thing like a bathmat. The more I found myself enjoying these minor pleasures, the more I began to realize that I needed this vacation. I needed a break from the stress of my life.

I padded out of the bathroom and headed into the closet, where I changed into a red sweater and jeans. When I got out, Em was standing in front of the door with her arms folded and her lips pursed. Her signature *I'm going to get what I want* move. I sighed as I stepped around her and over to the vanity, where I grabbed my brush and pulled my hair from the towel I'd twisted around it.

"I'm not going to leave you alone until you tell me," she said as she moved to stand next to me.

I sighed as I turned. "What do you want to know?"

Her excited smile instantly made me want to retract my statement, but I was too late. She caged my hands inside of hers and led me over to the bed. I sat down next to her, our knees bumping —we were that close.

Her eyes were wide as she peered into mine. I could tell she was ready, so I took in a deep breath. "Nothing much happened. We walked the sidewalks. Went to the bakery...crap." The bake-off. I sighed. Even though I wanted to call in sick, I knew I needed to show up. There was no way I was going to let Shelly think she won.

Em frowned. "What? Why crap?"

I sighed as I glanced around. "I agreed to enter a baking contest." I marked my statement with a moan.

"You did?" Em sounded a bit more excited that I'd expected.

"Yeah. When we were picking out doughnuts, there was some girl there who was glaring at me like she owned Ethan." Ugh. Why did I have to use those words? *I* didn't own Ethan, and yet the way I'd phrased it made it seem as if I thought I did. "I mean, Ethan is his own person and isn't owned by anyone."

Em looked confused for a moment before she shook her head. "There was a girl at the bakery?"

I turned back to working on my makeup. "Yes. Shelly." I hated how middle school I sounded when I said her name, but that was how I felt. Shelly annoyed me even though I'd just met her.

"And she roped you into a baking contest?" Em asked it slowly as if she were trying to piece together what had happened.

I nodded. "Yes. Why?"

Em's emerging smile had me instantly regretting our conversation. "It's perfect," she whispered as she moved to the mirror in the bathroom.

"Hang on, no, it's not," I said as I followed her. I was beginning to learn that *it's perfect* to Em was code for *Hallmark movie trope*. "It's not perfect. It was a coincidence. That is it."

Em was standing in front of the mirror, blotting her lipstick with some toilet paper. "Haven't you learned that there is no such thing as coincidence?" She turned to face me. "At least not here in Christmasland."

Here we go again. "This town is not trying to purposely give us a Hallmark movie experience." I leaned against the counter in the bathroom and studied her.

"Right. Sure," she said as she fluffed her hair. "And Porter and

Ethan just happened to make breakfast for two strangers." She gave me an unimpressed look.

"Well…yeah." I hated how uncertain I sounded. Why couldn't I be more confident about this? Did I really think that Ethan wanted to spend the morning with me? Did it seem more likely that he was being forced to do this by someone higher up in Christmasland? Was I delusional enough to think that he voluntarily wanted to spend time with me?

I wanted to say, no, I wasn't. That it just might be more likely for him to invite me to breakfast because he had to instead of him actually wanting to. But neither scenario made sense to me. First, he'd just met me—so there's no way he would be that interested. Second, there was definitely no scheme to give us a ridiculous holiday experience. This was just a town that loved Christmas and had found a way to monetize it.

Period.

I groaned as I buried my face in my hands. I needed to get out of my head.

"You're thinking too much. Whether it's fake or not, enjoy it. After all, in a few days we will return to normal life, and you'll regret it if you don't take advantage of every experience." She reached out and patted my arm. "That's what I'm doing."

I peeked through my fingers at her. Em looked so at ease that I felt jealous. Why couldn't I be like that? What did I have to over-think everything?

I was a rational person. Getting inside my own head had historically caused issues for me. I should remember that.

"So you think I should just go along with everything?"

Em nodded. "You'll have a good time, and that furrow" —she motioned toward my forehead— "will lessen."

I rubbed my brow. "I don't have a worry line."

She snorted. "Okay." Then she clapped her hands. "Finish getting ready. We're expected downstairs in a few minutes."

I sighed as I headed back to the mirror, where I attempted to keep my mind focused as I worked on finishing my makeup. I was just overthinking things, that was all. There was nothing for me to stress about. It wasn't like Ethan and I were destined for each other or anything.

I was here to have a fun and enjoyable vacation, and I was tired of getting in my own way. I could survive a picnic. I could even compete in a bake-off and live to tell the tale. I needed to stop focusing on things I couldn't explain and just live.

I could do that.

Fifteen minutes later, we were dressed and ready to go. I followed after Em as she led us out into the hallway and down the stairs. Ethan and Porter were standing in the foyer with their winter jackets and hats on. I tried to look relaxed as I walked up to Ethan with a smile.

"Hey," I said.

Ethan startled and then glanced down at me. His eyes widened, and I couldn't tell if it was because he was surprised I came or because he was happy to see me. Whichever it was, I wasn't going to worry about it. I was just going to take everything that came at me.

"We're ready," Em sang out as Porter grabbed her jacket from the hook and helped her slip it on.

Ethan looked out of place as he stood next to me. Then he stepped forward to grab my coat.

"I can get it," I said at the same time he said, "Let me get it."

We both stopped, and I peeked up at him. His skin looked flushed as he pinched his lips together.

"I can help you," he said quietly.

I nodded and watched as he pulled my coat—the right one this time—from the hook. Then he shook it a few times and held it up for me. I slipped my arms into the sleeves, and he pulled it up over my shoulders. I zipped my jacket and slipped on my gloves as Em clapped her hands and smiled at both Porter and Ethan.

"So where is this magical breakfast picnic happening?"

Porter linked arms with her, and they led the way out onto the porch. Not sure what to do, I offered my elbow to Ethan. He looked hesitant but then slipped his arm through mine. Warmth emanated from where we touched. And I hated that.

I hated that I didn't know if this was real or not. I hated that I couldn't prepare myself either way. And I hated that, deep down, I was starting to wish that this just might be real.

I gasped when we stepped out onto the porch and were met with the sight of two horses hitched to a sleigh. They were tied to the banister and were happily munching on some hay at their feet. I turned to stare at Ethan.

"Oh my gosh," Em said as she hurried down the stairs. "Is this for us?" Her squeal filled the air as she walked around the horses.

"Yep. It's going to take us to our picnic spot," Porter said as he followed after her.

I turned to look at Ethan. "Is he serious? Is this for us?"

Ethan glanced down at me, and a smile emerged. "My mom knows a guy. He let us borrow this for the morning." Then his expression shifted from happy to shy. "Is that okay?"

I blew out my breath. They were really leaning into this. "This is incredible. Porter did all of this for Em?" I slipped in that last sentence to see what he was going to say. Did he want to take me to breakfast, or was he just going along with Porter, who seemed enthralled with my friend? He didn't leave her side last night, and I couldn't help but assume that the letter was from Porter and not Ethan. It just didn't seem like something he would do.

Ethan furrowed his brow. "Are you asking if Porter planned this?"

I nodded.

Then he shrugged. "Would it matter if he did?"

I met his gaze. I wasn't sure what he was getting at. His expression was cloudy, and I was struggling to read it. "Not really."

Then he sighed. "It was a joint effort." He extended his hand toward the sleigh. "We should get going before Horace needs the horses back for the afternoon."

I nodded and headed down the stairs. I couldn't help but feel as if Ethan was upset with me. Was it wrong to wonder if he was doing this for me or just tagging along on something Porter planned for Em?

Even though I was trying to convince myself that I didn't need to know, I couldn't ignore the nagging in my mind. The more I got to know Ethan, the more I doubted everything I originally thought when I came to this town.

He wasn't being as direct as I wanted him to be. Which was bothering me.

We climbed into the sleigh, and Ethan took control of the reins. Em and Porter sat on the bench that faced out while I sat next to Ethan at the front. Even though I was agitated when I got in, it didn't take long before that anxiety melted away and I was left with the breathtaking views that played out in front of us.

The sun was shining through the trees and reflecting off the snow on the ground and on the branches. It was snowing slightly, and it looked as if glitter was falling around us. The green of the evergreen trees contrasted against the white, creating a combination that was calming in a way that I never thought possible.

I settled back on the bench and allowed my mind to relax.

Em was right. I didn't need answers right now. I was here to enjoy myself, and overthinking things was going to ruin my attempt at a vacation.

No matter what was happening, I could be happy if I let myself. I would enjoy this place for what it was and not think too deeply on the meaning. Then, I was guaranteed a good experience.

I didn't want to get hurt, and I feared that if I allowed myself to get to know Ethan more, that would be the inevitable outcome.

He may be here as part of an innocent ruse, but I was not.

And I needed to remember that.

11

ETHAN

Mom did not disappoint. After I scoured the internet last night, I went to her room at midnight declaring that I was going to kill four birds with one stone.

Mom looked rightfully confused as she sat up in bed and blinked. I felt bad for waking her up, but if I was going to give Beatrice the quintessential Christmas experience, I might as well start off with a bang. And that meant crossing *sleigh ride*, *Christmas breakfast*, *picnic*, and *handwritten letter* off the list.

Thankfully, Mom agreed to handle the food for me. If she hadn't, we would have been stuck with eating Raisin Bran and fruit. That was just about the only thing I could make.

Porter was on board. But I think it had more to do with the fact that he was still a part of this instead of his actual enthusiasm for what we were doing. When I got back to the inn this morning after having picked up the horses, I found him stretching his facial muscles in front of the foyer mirror.

It bothered me that he was so okay with faking all of this for Emilia and Beatrice. Even though I was doing the same, at least I was doing it to help Beatrice. Porter was doing it to help Porter.

So when Beatrice asked me if Porter planned this, I was disappointed that she didn't think me capable of creating this experience for her. But she didn't know my plan, so I couldn't really get upset with her. That wouldn't be fair.

I peeked over at her as I drove the horses deeper into the woods that surrounded the inn. Did she really think that I couldn't plan this for her? Was it really that hard to think that I knew what made a good Christmas outing?

I shook my head as I turned my focus back to the path that stretched out in front of us. I needed to stop thinking so much and just be here in the moment. I needed to stop worrying about what was going to happen when Beatrice left. If I could give her the Christmas that she never had, then I would have done my job.

It didn't take long before the trees parted, exposing a clearing. A firepit sat in the center, and picnic tables surrounded it. I clicked my tongue and shook the reins, directing the horses to the left. Once they couldn't go any further, they stopped and we all jumped down from the sleigh.

I contemplated hurrying over to Beatrice's side and helping her down, but she beat me to it. When her feet landed on the ground, she turned to grin at me. I wasn't sure what to make of the look in her eye. She looked happy, which was nice, but I couldn't stop the desire to see something deeper. Something more.

Was she feeling what I was feeling?

I was a dork.

I cleared my throat and nodded toward the back of the sleigh. "I'll get the food."

"I'll help," Beatrice said as she moved to follow me.

Emilia and Porter declared that they were going to get a fire started. I nodded, but my focus wasn't on them. It was on Beatrice. Her arm brushed mine as she leaned across the sleigh and pulled one of the insulated bags closer to her.

When she straightened, she flicked her hair over her shoulder and smiled up at me. "Got it."

I wasn't sure if it was the smell of her shampoo or her proximity as she stood next to me, but my whole brain felt foggy. My heart had picked up speed, and I was left blinking rapidly in an effort to get control of my body.

Beatrice's face entered my line of sight. She was frowning as her gaze raked over me. "You okay?" she asked.

I swallowed, forcing myself to wake up. If my mind didn't clear soon, I was going to head to Dr. Willow's office to have him check me out. I could be having a brain aneurysm with the way my body was acting.

"Yeah, I'm great," I said as I reached forward and pulled the last two bags toward me and then slipped them onto my shoulder. "Just lightheaded." I hurried to add, "Because I'm hungry."

Beatrice chuckled. "Low blood sugar?" Her smile was genuine and caused me to pause.

Not wanting to give away just what she was doing to me, I forced my body to keep moving. "Something like that."

When we got to the picnic table, I handed the bags over to Beatrice, so she could hold them while I brushed off the snow from the table and benches. Thankfully, Mom had enough foresight to pack us blankets to sit on.

Once the table was clean, Beatrice and I set out the containers of food while Porter stacked the wood in the pit and lit a fire. Soon the smell of Mom's ham quiche and the sound of crackling wood filled the air.

We settled down at the table and ate in silence. The food was so delectable that we didn't want any of it to cool before we could consume it.

I peeked over at Beatrice, who had sat next to me. It was strange. Even though we hadn't officially called this a double date, it seemed Emilia and Beatrice knew instinctively who was with whom. Emilia was laughing and swatting at Porter's arm as he told a joke, and Beatrice just smiled as she sat next to me.

This breakfast almost felt...normal.

If planning a Christmas breakfast like this was at all normal. Which it wasn't.

This wasn't me. Grand gestures didn't come naturally—and I had a slew of women I'd dated who would agree. I didn't know how to be the romantic type, and being here, pretending to be, felt like a lie.

Even though I felt like a fraud, Beatrice looked happy. So for now, I was going to be okay with that.

Our conversation remained light as we finished up the food. Emilia was teasing Porter, and they looked so at ease that I wondered if Beatrice and I were ever going to feel that way. How could my bum of a cousin connect with someone so effortlessly while I was struggling to string together three words?

I both hated and respected him for his ability at improv.

Emilia and Porter declared that they didn't care that it was breakfast time, they were going to roast the marshmallows Mom had packed. With them gone, the table was quiet, and I was desperate to engage Beatrice in some sort of conversation.

"Did you sleep well?" I asked.

She was mid sip on her hot chocolate. She finished swallowing and then set her cup down. "Yes, I did." She tucked her shoulders up to her ears. "It was how I would imagine sleeping at the North Pole actually goes."

I raised my eyebrows.

"I mean, if I were to stay in Santa's room, that's how I'd imagine it would feel."

I widened my eyes.

"That sounds wrong, doesn't it," she said as she giggled, "me sleeping in Santa's room."

I raised my hands. "Hey, you said it. I didn't."

She lifted her mug back up to her lips and took a sip. I could feel her gaze over the rim as she tipped the cup up. Then she squinted at me as she set the mug back down on the table.

I wasn't sure how I felt about her scrutinizing me. After all, I was acutely aware of my flaws, and the fact that she seemed intent to focus solely on me meant I wasn't going to be able to hide them. She was going to witness them if I didn't do something fast.

"I slept great. Thanks for asking." Except I hadn't. I spent the whole night tossing and turning. Partly because I was nervous about this morning and partly because of Porter's snoring.

She dabbed the sides of her mouth with her gloved hand. "I'm happy to hear that."

"You are?"

She met my gaze. "Of course. I need the judge for this afternoon to be well rested and awake."

"Judge?"

Her gaze lingered as she furrowed her brow. "You forgot already?"

"Forgot?" I racked my brain for what she was talking about. And then it dawned on me. I was judging the baking competition today. "Right...the bake-off."

"Well, I'm glad that you could forget, because I cannot." She set her arm down on the table and then leaned forward to rest her forehead on it. "It's going to be a disaster," she moaned.

"I'm sure you'll do great." I moved to pat her back but then decided against it. After all, I wasn't sure what was appropriate conduct for me in our relationship, and the last thing I needed was for a "very handsy" review to show up on our website.

So I set my clasped hands on the table and decided that was the best place for them.

Beatrice straightened and glanced over at me. She sighed as she blew her hair from her face. "I'm telling you, it's going to be a disaster." Her cheeks flushed as she leaned into me. I leaned back slightly, not sure if she realized how close we now were.

"When I was a kid, I thought I would try to make some bread. I'd watched on a kid show how to make bread with water and flour. Or at least, those were the only ingredients that I could remember." She closed her eyes and wrinkled her nose. "Bricks. That's what I made. I made bricks." She opened her eyes back up and offered me a goofy smile. "My poor foster dad. He felt bad that I was so upset, so he ate the half-baked goo."

I laughed, imagining Beatrice crying over bricks of flour and water. She swatted my arm as an exaggerated expression passed over her face. "It's not funny," she said with a pout.

I raised my hands. "Hey, I'm not the one that thought the way to make bread is by adding water to flour."

She playfully glowered at me. "Well, I know that now."

I chuckled. "That's good to know 'cause you're going to have to showcase that knowledge for half the town."

Her expression faltered. "Right."

Not wanting her to feel alone, I leaned in. This time, I didn't police how close I got or how long I lingered. I wanted to be closer to her, and every time we spoke, I grew more and more confident. "All right, I give in."

Beatrice stilled, and for a moment, I feared that I had over-stepped. I peered down at her, hoping she'd give me some signal as to what had caused her to freeze. Then, slowly, she turned her head so that she could meet my gaze.

"You do?" she asked, her voice barely a whisper.

For a moment, we just sat there, looking at each other. I wasn't sure if it was because she wanted to or if she was convinced that if she stared at me long enough, the answer to her question would appear on my forehead.

Realizing that I was most likely reading more into her reaction than she'd intended, I smiled and nodded. "I do." She still looked confused, so I added, "I'll help you."

"Help me?"

This was the strangest conversation. "Yes. I will help you bake today."

She shook her head. "Is that ethical? After all, you are a judge."

"Let's call it self-preservation. I don't want to eat glue." I held up my hands. "But I promise that you will be the one doing most of the work. I'll just be behind the scenes to guide you."

She eyed me and then sighed. "I get to do what I want?" she asked, raising her finger just in front of my face and wiggling it.

I raised my right hand. "I swear."

She pursed her lips to the side, and then a smile slowly emerged. "Fine. Deal. I'll take your help," she said.

I nodded, and just before I could respond, Porter and Emilia returned to the table with roasted marshmallows on their sticks.

"What's going on over here?" Emilia asked as she sat down on the bench and began to pull off the browned bits of marshmallow and slip them into her mouth.

"Ethan kindly offered to help me with the bake-off this afternoon." Beatrice said it so nonchalantly that I glanced down at her. I don't know what I was expecting, but deep down, part of me hoped that she would sound a little more excited.

"He did?" Emilia asked with more emphasis that one would expect.

"Em," Beatrice said. Her voice was lower now, and I could tell she was staring intently at her friend.

Emilia raised her hands. "I didn't say anything." When she lowered her hands, her smile remained. "I just think it's sweet." She gave a subtle wink to Beatrice, who just sighed.

"Anyway, we should probably get back, huh? Your mom is probably wondering where her helper is, and I need to figure out what I'm going to make." Beatrice began clearing the table. After the now empty containers were returned to the bags, she turned to nod toward the horses. "Ready?"

I helped Porter kick snow on the fire and the flames fizzled to steam. Once we were sure it was out for good, we climbed back onto the sleigh, and I clicked my tongue to wake up the horses. They neighed and began pulling us back to the inn.

Beatrice sighed as she leaned back and closed her eyes. The sun shone down on her skin, and I couldn't help but stare at her long neck and creamy skin. I wanted to reach out and touch it—but I resisted. I wasn't a creep, but these desires were causing me to doubt myself.

"Did you enjoy breakfast?" I asked as I focused on the trail in front of us. I didn't want her to see that a lot of my hopes rested on what she was about to say.

She chuckled. I was getting used to the sound. It was soft and low, and it sent shivers across my skin. I'd never realized how rewarding a smile and laugh could be until I heard hers.

"I did." Then suddenly, she leaned in. I tensed as I waited for her to rest her head on my shoulder, that was how close she was. "Thank you," she whispered before moving back to her seat.

My heart was pounding so loud that I could hear it in my ears. I swallowed as I willed my body to return to normal. She was just thanking me for breakfast. I was the idiot who'd allowed myself to hope that something different was going to happen.

That wasn't why I was here in the first place. I wanted to give Beatrice the Christmas she never got as a kid, not get her to fall for me. Plus, I wasn't in a place where I could entertain the thought of any kind of relationship.

I was broken, and from what she'd told me about her past, the last thing she needed was a broken man. I needed to be okay with that.

If I wanted to do what was best for Beatrice, I was going to get control of my emotions right now. Before I did something I regretted and negated all the good I was doing for her.

She deserved better, and I was determined to give her that.

No matter what.

12

BEATRICE

"Let me get this straight, he *offered* to help you bake for the
competition?" Em asked as she followed me around our
room.

I frowned at her use of air quotes when she said *offered*.

I wasn't going to lie, I was on cloud nine since our breakfast.
Ethan was especially doting when we got back to the inn, helping
me out of the sleigh and allowing his hand to linger for a moment
longer than was appropriate if we were just friends. He didn't
meet my gaze to verify what I thought as I stood there holding his
hand, but I wasn't going to read into it.

After all, I was trying take a page out of Em's book and just
allow myself to enjoy what was happening as it happened. There
was no need to obsess about whether Ethan experienced the same
zaps of electricity that rushed through my hand from his touch.
Because it didn't matter. I was here, and I was going to allow this
vacation to roll out as it needed to.

I sighed. "It's not a big deal. It's just a baking competition.
You're making it sound like he made a declaration of love or
something." I gave her an annoyed look, but if she saw it, she
didn't acknowledge it.

"He's good," she said under her breath.

That comment caused me to stop. "What does that mean?" I asked as I stared her down.

Em studied me and then shook her head. "Never mind." She blew out her breath. "I'm excited for you. You're going to have fun."

I stared at her for a moment longer and then nodded. "I know. I'm trying to relax and enjoy myself. And I think Ethan can help me do that."

"Of course. Then that's what you need to do."

I glanced at the clock. I had five minutes before I needed to meet Ethan downstairs, so I hurried to slip my shoes on. "Behave while I'm gone, okay? Once the baked good is out of the oven, I'll find you, so we can head into town. The bake-off starts at one."

Em gave me a stiff salute, and I just laughed as I made my way over to the door and stepped out into the hall.

The inn was quiet except for the soft Christmas music that played over the speakers. I sighed as I paused in the foyer and glanced around. The smells, the sounds, all of it was growing on me. Christmasland was turning out to be exactly what it boasted it was. A place where time stilled, and the holidays flourished.

"Are you looking for something?" Carol's voice sounded from behind me.

I startled and turned, pressing my hand to heart. "Oh, you scared me," I said.

She gave me a sheepish smile. "Sorry. They don't call me feather foot for no reason." She motioned toward her reindeer slippers.

"Ah," I said, not sure how to respond to that. Remembering her question, I motioned toward the back, where I assumed the kitchen was. "I'm looking for Ethan. He promised to help coach me as I make something for the bake-off in town."

Carol's eyes widened, and I hoped that she was more surprised that Ethan was helping me and less that it was *me* who was baking. I knew my cooking was bad, but it wasn't like it was legendary.

"He did? Well, isn't that nice," she said as she patted my forearm. "Follow me. I'll show you where the kitchen is.

We weaved through the dining room and pushed through a swinging door that led into a fully stocked kitchen. It was cluttered but in an organized way. If I had a grandmother, I would want her kitchen to look like this. Pots hung from the ceiling, as well as different herbs that were drying.

"This is incredible," I said as I reached out and ran my hand along the smooth marble countertops.

"Thanks. When Steve died, I struggled to pull out of my depression. Ethan was worried about me. He would call home every day to make sure that I made myself food and showered." She glanced over at me as an embarrassed expression passed over her face. "I'm so sorry. TMI."

I shrugged. "I understand. I lost my parents when I was just a baby, so I know loss."

"You did?"

I hated that a lump rose up in my throat every time I talked about my history. It wasn't like it was new to me. It wasn't like I had any other story to tell. "My parents abandoned me," I said in the most nonchalant tone I could muster.

"I'm so sorry," she whispered as she reached out and covered my hand with hers. And then, slowly, her expression morphed into one of concern. "What did you do for the holidays?"

I shrugged. "It depended on what my foster family wanted to do. Some celebrated, some didn't." I pushed around a few crumbs on the counter as I waited for Carol to respond. I was fairly certain how she would react, and I wasn't sure if I was ready for it.

"I'm so sorry," she said as she leaned in and wrapped me in a hug. "Every child should experience Christmas." Her voice was cracking as if she were on the verge of tears.

Her reaction only spurred on my own response. I didn't want to cry, but with her hugging me as tight as she was, I feared she would squeeze the tears out despite my efforts to keep them inside.

"It's okay," I said as I patted her back.

Carol hugged me for a bit longer before she pulled away. I was surprised to see her expression had changed from sad to resolute. "It's settled," she said as she dusted off her hands.

"What's settled?" I didn't like the determined tone to her voice or the crazed look in her eyes.

Carol waved off my question as she hurried over to the far wall. She disappeared into another room and shut the door behind her. I stood there, staring at the spot she'd been in just moments ago, confused as to what had just happened.

"Everything okay?" Ethan's deep voice caused me to jump. I turned to see that he was holding an apron in each hand and was studying me.

"What?" I asked before I could stop myself. Why was I so jumpy, and why did my voice come out so weak?

"I asked if everything is okay. You're just staring off into space with a confused look on your face."

Not wanting to go over what had just happened between his mom and me, I motioned toward the aprons. "Is one of these for me?"

He furrowed his brow but didn't push me further. Instead, he nodded and handed me one. "Yep."

I took it and slipped it on. Just when I went to tie it, Ethan moved to step behind me. "I can help," he offered.

His fingers brushed mine, and suddenly, I forgot how to even move my hands. I hesitated but then slipped my hands out of the way, and he proceeded to tie the strings. His body was so close to mine that I could feel his warmth cascade across my back. I could feel his presence without actually being touched by him.

It was completely overwhelming and relaxing at the same time.

As soon as he was done, I took a giant step forward just to give myself space from him. I was ready to get this baking experience over with and move on with my day, preferably very far away from Ethan and Carol. My emotions seemed to veer off track whenever they came around.

I clapped my hands. "I'm ready. What should I make?"

Ethan studied me. His arms were folded across his chest and he was leaning against the countertop with his legs extended. A smile played on his lips that drew my attention up to his mouth. For a moment, a very slight moment, I wondered what it would be like to kiss him. And then reality slapped me in the face, and I turned so my back was to him while I gathered together what little self-control I had.

"What do you like? Bread? Cookies? Rolls?" Ethan's voice grew louder, and I could see from the corner of my eye that he was approaching me.

Needing something to do other than think about where he was and if he was going to touch me, I moved to open the cupboards as if I were looking for inspiration.

"I like cookies," I said softly as I ran through the list he'd sounded off.

"Cookies are good." He was standing behind me. I felt tiny in his presence. He wouldn't even need to move to the side to see around me. All he had to do was stand there and he could see over me.

"Cookies it is." I tapped my chin. "Now, what kind?"

"What's your favorite?"

I pursed my lips. I knew the fight over which cookie was best was as old as time, and I wasn't sure what Ethan would say if I told him what I personally liked. Then, realizing that I was being stupid, I said, "Oatmeal raisin."

When he didn't respond, I glanced over my shoulder to see

him staring down at me. His eyebrows were raised, and I couldn't quite read his expression. Was he officially disgusted by me? How did I fix this?

"Really?" he asked.

I nodded. There was no way I was going to be able to rewind time and take it back, so I might as well fully embrace my answer. "I love how soft they are, and the texture..." My mouth started to water at the thought.

"All right. Oatmeal raisin it is." He leaned forward, his chest brushing my shoulder. My entire body tensed until he pulled back with a package of raisins in his hand.

"Let's get started then," he said as he turned around and set the container down on the counter.

I pulled up a recipe on my phone and read out the ingredients to Ethan as he moved around the kitchen and grabbed what I called off. Soon, everything was laid out in a line on the counter.

Just as Ethan grabbed the mixer to bring it to where we were working, Carol emerged from her office. She was holding a binder to her chest and smiled at us as she walked by. I wondered what she was doing, but she was gone before I could ask.

I made a mental note to ask Ethan what my interaction with her had been about. I doubted he knew, but I figured it wouldn't hurt to ask.

"Ready?" Ethan asked. I turned to see him waving a measuring cup in my face.

Nervousness exploded in my stomach, but I attempted to push it down. After all, it was just cookies. What could be complicated about them?

I took the measuring cup and moved to stand next to him. "All right. You read the instructions and I'll mix the ingredients."

Ethan sucked in his breath. I turned to see that his cheeks were puffed out as he stared down at me. "I'm not sure that's exactly ethical," he said after he let his breath out in a solid puff.

I gave him an annoyed look. "It's not unethical. You're just reading." Then I rested my hand on my hip. "Are you telling me that recipes aren't your preferred go-to material?"

He chuckled as he pulled up a nearby stool and sat down. "Only when I feel really dangerous do I read recipes." He pulled open the raisins and grabbed a handful. On instinct, I swatted his hand away.

His jaw dropped, and heat flushed my cheeks when I realized what I'd done. This wasn't my kitchen or house. If anything, he had more right to the raisins than I did. What was wrong with me?

"I'm so sorry," I stammered.

Ethan's shocked expression morphed to a smile as he slid off the stool and reached into the jar of flour. "Oh, it's on now," he said as he flicked the flour in my direction.

I shrieked and ducked out of the way, but when I glanced down, I noticed I was caked in flour. I stayed crouched down by the countertop but slipped my hand onto the counter in search of ammunition. I found the flour and grabbed a handful before the jar was slid away from me.

"What are you doing?" Ethan asked.

I clenched my fist around the flour and then popped up from where I hid just to have another blast of flour cover my shirt. Not wanting to miss my opportunity to land a blow while he had no ammo, I threw it at him. It coated his face, hair, and clothes.

Ethan stood there with his mouth open and a crazed look in his eye as he stared at me with his flour-covered face. "No fair. Faces should be off limits."

I giggled as I reached out to grab a nearby kitchen towel. "I'm so sorry. I wasn't aware of the etiquette that came with a food fight," I said as I stepped forward with the towel outstretched.

He studied me for a moment before he pinched his lips and leaned in as if he wanted me to wipe the flour from his face. My heart began to pound inside of my chest as my gaze roamed his.

He looked welcoming and relaxed as if this was as natural as breathing.

Which was a startling contrast to the nerves racing through me. Where he looked calm, I felt like a racehorse had taken off inside of me. But he looked expectant, and I didn't want to be the fish out of water in this situation, so I stepped forward and brought the towel up to his face.

I began brushing the flour off only to notice that Ethan hadn't taken his gaze off me for a moment. He was staring at me with such intensity that the world around me began to spin.

Was I reading this wrong? Was it real? Fake?

I wasn't sure. Em's voice kept echoing in my mind about how there were no coincidences, that everything at Christmasland was manufactured. But could that be true? The look in Ethan's eyes seemed genuine. I could feel his desire in the way he studied me. In his slight smile as he leaned closer.

I wanted to believe that this was the truth. But could I?

"Thank you," Ethan said. His voice had dropped low and husky.

I nodded as I continued wiping his face. "Of course. I mean, I did this to you, after all."

He chuckled. "That's true."

A silence fell over us, and I continued to work.

"Are you enjoying your stay at the North Pole?"

I paused to meet his gaze. There was a fire in the way he looked at me that made my stomach flip. I wanted to lean in. I wanted to let my worries go and just experience this vacation like Em was. With no strings or expectations. But I wasn't sure if I was capable of doing that.

"Yes," I whispered when I realized that I hadn't answered him. "I am."

His smile widened, and my gaze instantly dropped to his mouth. The desire to feel his lips pressed against mine raged inside of me. Suddenly, he straightened and moved closer. I glanced up to see that his gaze had intensified.

"Beatrice," he said softly.

I winced at his use of my full name. "Bea," I said quietly. I didn't move backward when he stepped closer to me. Did he want to kiss me like I wanted to kiss him? When I saw his gaze drift down to my mouth and then back up to lock with mine, I knew what he wanted. It was exactly what I had been fighting.

Slowly, his hand found my waist and slipped to my lower back. He held me there as he inched closer. I didn't move. It was a mixture of worry and joy that kept me rooted to the spot.

Perhaps I feared that if I moved or spoke, I would wake up. The last thing I wanted was to discover that I had fallen asleep in my apartment in New York and all of this had been a dream.

I did not want Ethan to be a dream.

I hesitated, but then I gathered my strength and rested my hands on his chest. I could feel his heart beating. It raced along with mine. That brought me a small level of satisfaction. He was as nervous as I felt.

Suddenly, he was lowering his head, and I stood there with my face tipped up to his, waiting for the kiss...

...that never came.

Instead, he jumped away from me as Carol came walking into the kitchen. She stopped, her gaze moving from me over to Ethan. "I'm sorry for interrupting," she stammered.

Ethan shoved his hands through his hair and shook his head. "You're not. I was just getting the flour off her...face." He winced as the last word left his lips.

I was no expert, but I was fairly certain that Carol didn't believe a word her son said. Her cheeks flushed, and she lifted the binder up as she passed by us. "I didn't see anything," she called over her shoulder as she disappeared into the room she'd left earlier.

Once she was gone, I blew out my breath. Not sure if I should look at Ethan or not, I decided it was better to just pull the bandage off. Sure, I was fairly certain that he'd been about to kiss me moments ago, but now? I didn't know where we stood.

And with his mom in the other room and the baking competition looming over me, I decided that that conversation could be tabled for another time.

Needing to move on, I dusted the flour from my apron and stepped up to the ingredients.

"Let's make some cookies."

13

ETHAN

I was in some deep water. No matter what I did or how hard I tried to stay away from Bea, I couldn't help but find myself right next to her. She was like a magnet for me.

It didn't help that our almost kiss was seared into my brain. Every time I looked at her, all I could see was her tipping her face toward me. All I could focus on was the curvature of her lips and what they might feel like pressed against mine.

What had started out as a playful event quickly turned intense when she stood next to me, sucking me in. And if I were completely honest with myself, I wanted all of this. I wanted her. I wanted us. And I wanted to be here with her experiencing Christmas this way.

I didn't want to admit it, but Christmasland was beginning to grow on me. It was fun, making these moments happen for Bea. She deserved them, and I wanted to give them to her. Probably more than I'd wanted anything else lately.

I leaned forward on the counter and watched as she pulled the last tray of cookies from the oven. The smell of melted sugar and cinnamon filled the air. I was surprised at her ability to tweak a recipe to make it her own.

For all her talk of not being a good baker, I was actually excited to taste what she created. Even though I was supposed to be an impartial judge, I could tell that these cookies had potential to win on their merit alone.

"Ouch," she said as she pulled her hand away quickly and brought her fingertips to her lips.

I was standing and making my way toward her before I could stop myself. "Everything okay?" I asked as I stepped up next to her and gently took her hand, so I could inspect it.

Bea's eyes were wide as she studied me. Then she nodded slowly. "Yeah. I just burned my fingers."

Ignoring the sensation that rushed through my body as my hand held hers, I nodded toward the sink. "Let's get some cold water on it." I hated how my voice deepened when she was around. It was out of instinct, but regardless, I knew she could sense the change in me. And right now, I wasn't sure I was ready to appear that vulnerable.

"Sure," she said as she followed me.

I flipped the faucet on and stuck her fingers under the running water. Her arm was pressed against my chest, and for a moment, I allowed myself to glance down at her. She was staring straight forward, and I couldn't tell if it was because she was interested in something outside the window or if she was trying to keep from looking at me.

With her hesitation to meet my gaze, I allowed myself to linger on her features. She was truly beautiful. Her lashes were long, and her skin was pale. I could see a dash of freckles across her nose and I wondered if those freckles darkened in the summer sun.

Would I even see her in the summer?

No. Of course not.

This was a vacation for her, and very few people wanted to go to Christmasland when it was a hundred degrees out.

Realization that I was allowing myself to get close to a person who I was most likely never going to see again hit Santa on the rooftop. So much so, that I loosened my grip on her hand and stepped back.

Why was I doing this to myself? I was here to get away from a woman who broke my heart, not find a replacement to do the same. If I wanted to heal, I needed to stop jumping feetfirst into everything.

"I think you'll be okay," I said after I put some distance between me and Bea.

She was wiggling her fingers under the water as she turned to look at me. She pinched her lips and nodded. "Thanks. They feel better already."

I grabbed a nearby dish towel and tossed it to her. She caught it, turned off the water, and then dabbed her fingers dry.

"Are they ready?" I asked, nodding toward the cookies that were laid out on Mom's cooling racks.

"I think so," she said softly as she blew out her breath.

"They look great."

Bea scoffed. "You have to say that because you kind of helped me. It's like a parent calling their baby beautiful. You created it, so of course you'd think it's great." But despite her words, I saw her cheeks flush as she dropped her gaze. My compliment had hit its mark.

"Well, I'm sure I won't be the only one who thinks that when we get to the bake-off." My gaze landed on the clock above the stove and panic set it. "Which we'll be late for if we don't leave now."

Bea's eyes widened as she glanced up at me. "We're going to be late?"

I nodded as I started riffling through the cupboards and then triumphantly emerged with a container. "This'll work," I said as I set it down on the countertop next to the cookies.

We spent the next five minutes gathering the cookies together and rinsing the dishes. Mom emerged from her office and told us not to worry about cleaning and to hurry up or Bea would be disqualified.

We nodded, and I ushered Bea through the door and out to the foyer. Emilia and Porter were milling around the living room. Emilia must have seen Bea's panicked expression because her smile instantly turned into a frown as she hurried over.

"Everything okay?" she asked.

Bea nodded. "Yeah. We're just going to be late if we don't get out of here."

Emilia tossed Bea her jacket and then grabbed her own. "I'm ready."

Porter declared that he was coming too, and before I could stop the raging river that was Emilia and Porter, they were out the door and down the stairs. I sighed as I shut the front door behind me and hurried after them. I should have known my intimate moment with Bea was over. Reality was back and more painful than ever.

The drive into town was filled with chatter. Emilia was going on and on about how good Bea's cookies smelled and how she was certain that Bea was going to be the winner. Porter was sitting in the passenger seat next to me and kept trying to engage me in conversation—but I wasn't really paying attention.

All I could do when I wasn't watching the road was allow my gaze to slip back to Bea. She really looked happy, and that made my chest swell. It felt good, being a part of all of this. She deserved to have the quintessential Christmas experience, and I could see her hesitant reaction against Christmasland start to lessen.

I pulled into the parking lot next to the Main Street park and turned off the engine. Emilia was still chatting with Bea as they both climbed out of the car and started off toward the gazebo, where the snow had been cleared and tables had been set up.

I slammed my door at the same time Porter did. I glanced over to see him hurry to catch up with me. I didn't want to make small talk on our way over to the event, but he looked determined, so I slowed just enough for him to fall into step with me.

He glanced over at me with a smile that I couldn't quite read.

"What?" I asked.

He shook his head. "Nothing." He fell silent for a moment before he sucked in his breath. "Are things going well?"

I knew it wasn't nothing. That kid always got ahead of himself. "What?" I asked again.

Porter waved toward Bea and Emilia. "Things seem to be going well, wouldn't you agree?"

I allowed my gaze to linger on Bea for a moment before I glanced over at Porter and shook my head. "I don't know what you're talking about."

Porter looked unconvinced. "Right. Sure," he said, but the smile on his face told me a different story.

I wanted to fight him to tell him that his assumption was incorrect, but Shelly spotted me and was headed my way before I could get my rebuttal out. Not wanting her to hear any of this, I shoved those thoughts far back in my mind and turned my focus to Shelly's bright eyes and flushed cheeks.

"You're here," she said as she linked arms with me and began to pull me toward the table with a large banner that read *Judges* taped to the front. "I was worried you'd forgotten."

I lifted my arm to push my hair from my face and to break her hold on me. I hated that she seemed to think she had the right to drag me around.

"I'm here now," I said as I nodded to the other judges, some of whom I recognized and some I didn't.

Shelly clapped her hands, effectively halting my response, and glanced around the group. "Great. Well, now that you are all here, let's go over the responsibility of the judges."

For the next five minutes, we were subject to Shelly as she read through the handbook. It was a little ridiculous that there was a whole binder to say, eat the food and judge the food accordingly, but who was I to say anything? Shelly looked distracted enough to stay away from me, and I was going to eat delicious foods, so it really was a win-win.

Once she was finished with the expectations, we all took a seat. I glanced around at the contestants, who were all standing behind their creations. I instantly found Bea. She was smiling and listening to Emilia, who was quite animated about what she was saying. I couldn't hear her, but I could tell, whatever it was, she was passionate about it.

Shelly welcomed everyone to the bake-off and said a few words. I was barely paying attention to what she was saying. Instead, I was attempting not to stare at Bea by scanning the crowd.

Everyone was decked out in either holiday attire or jackets and hats. It wasn't a subzero day, but it was chilly and the light breeze wasn't helping. Just as I finished inspecting the crowd, my gaze landed on a familiar face.

Worried that I was just seeing things, I narrowed my eyes to get a better look. And then my entire body went ice cold.

There, standing among the crowd, was...Scarlet.

Our gazes locked, and she smiled. It was soft and inviting and exactly what had gotten me into trouble the first go-around. She had a way of bewitching me like no other woman had. And it wasn't a good kind of bewitching. Her hold over me was one of control and manipulation.

The entire world tilted to the side, and in order to feel more in control, I dropped my gaze to the table and took in a deep breath. She wasn't here. I was just imagining things. I just needed to get through this bake-off, and then I could head back home to hole up in my room until I no longer imagined that Scarlet was here.

Shelly declared the start of the bake-off and then stepped off the stage. She waved to the first baker to bring up their entry. They stood in front of us and gave us a brief summary of what they made. I wasn't listening. Instead, my gaze kept slipping over to Scarlet, who hadn't moved from her spot.

Her red lips kept tipping up into a somewhat knowing smile. She even nodded when I met her gaze, and my stomach flip-flopped. She was here, and she wanted to see me.

This was a mistake.

Not wanting to make a scene or leave just to have Scarlet follow me, I forced myself to focus on the baked goods in front of me. I shoveled the food in and rated each contestant as best I could despite how confused I felt.

By the time we got to Bea, I felt sick, not only from the food, but also from the emotional tilt-a-whirl I'd just been placed on. My gaze met hers, and she looked confused as she studied me. Then she smiled, and I offered her a meager one in return.

"I decided to keep it simple today," she said as she slowly walked the table, holding the plate of cookies out. "Oatmeal raisin cookies always remain soft and can make the perfect Santa treat." She offered us a shy smile as if she was pleased with her joke.

I began to relax in her presence. She had a way of calming me. I wanted her around me now more than ever. She was the steadfast lighthouse in the storm that was my mind right now.

I kept my focus on her as I began to eat the cookie. The soft cinnamon taste exploded in my mouth. She'd insisted on soaking the raisins in apple juice, and that took the cookies to a whole new level. I could hear the murmurs of adoration from the other judges.

Bea looked concerned, but I made a point to give her an encouraging smile when her gaze met mine. Her cheeks flushed, but she pinched her lips together and nodded. I liked seeing her confidence grow as she scanned the judges. She was down on herself because of her baking mishaps in the past, but from what I was tasting right now, those feelings were not justified.

Bea finished and left the judging area. Although my distraction was gone, I felt better. If Bea could face her fears and participate in a bake-off where she felt out of her depth, then I could survive the sudden appearance of my ex.

I could be strong, and right now, I was determined to be.

Scarlet was here, sure. But that didn't mean I had to let her control me. I could be a strong person if I let myself be strong. I could conquer the pain my ex gave me, and I was going to do that, with the help of Bea.

I just needed to get her on board, first.

14

BEATRICE

I stood next to our table with my hands clasped in front of me, watching the judges as they deliberated. I felt sweaty and nervous as I watched them talk in hushed tones. If only I could read lips, I could figure out what they were saying.

"You okay?" Em asked me, snapping me from my concentration.

I glanced over and offered her a sheepish smile when I realized that I had been caught. "Yeah, I'm good," I said, blowing out my breath.

What was wrong with me? I hadn't realized how much I cared about this competition. After all, I sucked at baking, so why did I have this desire to win? I tipped my face toward the sky and closed my eyes.

I knew the reason, even if I didn't want to admit it. The truth was, I needed a win. For so long, my life had just been mediocre. There wasn't anything particularly special about me. And sure, winning a small-town bake-off wasn't the same as becoming a New York Times bestselling author, but it was a start. And right now, I needed a start.

I'd allowed myself to get my hopes up when I saw the reaction the judges had to my cookie. They'd looked pleased, and some even finished the entire thing—something they hadn't done for other competitors. And that response lit a small fire of hope in my chest that I just might pull off a win.

Plus, the pleased smile from Ethan spurred that hope on even more.

Movement by the judges table caught my attention. They peeled apart from the discussion they were having, and an older gentleman made his way over to Shelly and handed her an envelope. She smiled as she took it and then walked up to the microphone.

"The judges have picked their winners!" she announced as if she were on *The Price is Right*.

A hush fell over the crowd, and I felt myself hold my breath. Then, feeling like a dork, I released that breath and focused on making sure I breathed normally. This was just a baking competition. It wasn't the rest of my life.

"For second place…" Shelly paused and glanced around. This woman was clearly having way too much fun. "Tilly Langcaster."

There was a cheer from my left as a petite brown-haired woman, who looked about my age, made her way up to the stage. I could only assume that it was her family who was whooping and hollering as she accepted her gift card and small bouquet of flowers.

Once she was back with her family, Shelly returned to the piece of paper.

"For first place…" Again with the pausing. I rolled my eyes and glanced over at Em, but she was too busy chatting with Porter to see my reaction. I studied them, and for a moment, I wished Ethan was down here with us. He would have met my eyeroll with equal annoyance. And that felt strange to think. He'd been just a stranger not long ago, but now, now I felt as if he understood me.

Was that possible?

"Carter Paige," Shelly called out, and the cheering snapped me from my thoughts. I watched as a man walked up to the stage, got his prize, and left.

"Now, for the grand prize of a fifty-dollar gift card to Sugarplum Bakery. Plus an evening out at Snowtop Lane, all expenses paid. The winner is..."

A man next to us began to pound the table like a drummer. Shelly gave him an appreciative smile and then scanned the crowd. She paused and then announced, "Beatrice Thompson."

Em jumped up and began cheering. Porter looked startled but then joined in. Everyone around us looked confused, but then when they realized it was me, they began clapping and cheering.

I just stood there, shocked that I had heard my name. Did she mean me? Really?

"Beatrice, are you out there?" Shelly asked.

My cheeks flushed as I began to weave my way through the crowd. When I got to Shelly, she gave me an annoyed look as she passed over the bouquet of flowers and gift cards.

"Well played," she said as she leaned in and gave me a kiss on the cheek.

I stared at her, startled by her gesture and comment. "What?"

Shelly just grinned as she posed for a picture. "Your whole *I can't bake routine*." She glanced down at me. "Well played."

I wanted to tell her that I hadn't lied. I was a terrible baker, and this had happened due to sheer luck. But I didn't have time to respond as she stepped back, and all the judges moved to surround me. They gave handshakes and congratulations. Not sure what to say, I just nodded in response.

When I got to Ethan, his expression was hard to read. It was a mixture of excitement and nerves. For a moment there, he even looked as if he'd seen a ghost.

"Congrats," he said as he leaned in and managed a smile. Even though he felt distant, he looked as if he were trying to force himself out of the funk he was in. And I appreciated it.

Although it did confuse me. Especially since I was fairly certain he'd wanted to kiss me earlier in the kitchen. But perhaps, I was the only one who'd felt the fire that burned between us when he held me close and lowered his lips to mine...

"Bea?"

I blinked a few times, pulling myself from that memory. What was wrong with me? Why was I daydreaming about kissing him?

It was official, I'd lost my mind.

"Yeah?" I asked as Ethan entered my line of sight.

"You okay?"

I nodded as I held the bouquet of flowers closer to my chest. The movement made the flowers shift, and I was suddenly met with the sweetest smell. They were beautiful.

"You looked a little shocked," he said as he folded his arms across his chest.

"I'm not shocked. I mean, I am a closet baker." I waggled my finger in his direction. "I pulled the wool over your eyes, didn't I?"

He held up his hands. "You're right. I did not see the plot twist."

I smiled, relieved that whatever was going on between us didn't stop us from teasing each other. It felt almost therapeutic to stand there teasing him. I needed this. Especially after our intense moment in the kitchen. I needed to know that we could still be what I was beginning to love about us.

Friends.

"Hey, Ethan," a sugary sweet voice said. We both turned, and Ethan instantly tensed.

I peeked over at the woman. Who was she to get Ethan to react like this?

"I hope it's okay that I came."

So this woman had a past with Ethan. She was tall and thin. She wasn't dressed in the festive gear most tourists wore. Instead she had on a long black peacoat, and her hair was pulled up into a tight bun on the top of her head. Her lips were a deep red, and her makeup seemed perfect.

I was an ugly duckling in her presence. Even though I was fairly certain that we were the same age, I felt like a child as I stood next to her in my fur-lined boots and oversized jacket.

When Ethan didn't respond, I glanced over at him and then back to the woman. Ethan looked frozen in place, so I reached my hand out.

"I'm Beatrice," I said with a smile.

She flicked her gaze over to me and then down to my hand. I could tell that the last thing she wanted was to shake my hand. But I wasn't going to be intimidated by her. I was, after all, the Christmasland bake-off grand prize winner.

She seemed to realize that I wasn't going to drop my hand, so she took it gingerly with her leather-gloved hand. "Scarlet," she said.

I should have known. A woman that pretentious obviously came with a pretentious-sounding name.

"Nice to meet you, Scarlet," I said as I brought my hand back to hug the bouquet of flowers. "Is this your first time at Christmasland?"

She didn't look as if she wanted to engage in conversation, but since Ethan was still frozen, she sighed and focused on me.

"Yes. It is."

I nodded. "Me, too," I said as I leaned in.

She gave me a smug smile and then focused back on Ethan.

"Are you visiting family?"

She sighed and glanced back at me. "No."

"On vacation then?" Ethan needed to snap out of whatever stupor he was in. I could only keep this small chat going for so long.

"No." Then her smile widened. "I'm here to see Ethan. Now, if you'll excuse us, I'd like to talk to him in private."

Ethan paled at her words, and the desire to help him rushed through me. I needed to step in, now.

"Nah," I said before I could come up with a more eloquent response.

Her perfectly formed eyebrows rose. "Nah?"

My cheeks flushed. "I mean, I'm good. I'm staying." I'd wanted to sound confident, but my voice just came out weak. Why wasn't I a stronger person?

"You're staying?"

I linked arms with Ethan. That seemed to wake him up. He glanced down at me and then to our linked arms.

"Yeah," I said as I glanced up to meet Ethan's gaze. He looked panicked, so I allowed the next few words to emerge before I gave them further thought. "That's what a good girlfriend does."

Ethan's lips parted, and his eyebrows went up. I could tell that he wanted to correct me, so I gave him a *go with it* look.

"Girlfriend?" Scarlet asked.

Ethan stared at me for a moment before he nodded and glanced up at her. "Yeah. Girlfriend." Then he narrowed his eyes. I moved to lay my head on his shoulder. I wanted to say that my display of affection was forced, but the truth was, I was beginning to like Ethan.

Like, a lot.

"Wow. That was...fast." Scarlet glanced around as she fidgeted. I could tell she felt uncomfortable, and I took that as a win.

"What are you doing here?" Ethan asked.

He seemed to have found his confidence, and I wanted to cheer when I heard the bite in his tone. Even though I didn't know their history, I was beginning to piece things together.

Scarlet sighed. "I came to see you."

I felt Ethan tense up, but I didn't let him go. Whoever she was, I wasn't going to let her manipulate him.

"Why would you do that?"

Scarlet took a step forward. I could tell she wanted to say

something, but when her gaze met mine, she pinched her lips. After a moment, she said, "Can I speak with you tonight?" And then she added, "Alone?"

When Ethan didn't respond right away, I glanced up at him. Was he seriously considering meeting with her? Didn't he know how those kinds of meetings went? She was obviously his big-city ex-girlfriend who had followed him back to his hometown to beg for his forgiveness. I'd seen the movies. I knew how this played out.

She was here to get him back, and he seemed to be playing right into her hand.

"I can do that," he said. His voice was low, and I could tell that he was struggling.

"Darling," I said before I could stop myself. Ethan glanced down at me. I made sure my smile was wide as I stared up at him. "Don't you remember? We're going to Snowtop Lane tonight." I reached up and patted his cheek. "Silly."

Ethan's eyebrows rose. "We are?"

I nodded. "Yes," I said as I snuggled into his shoulder.

"It won't take long. I swear." Scarlet held up her hand. Her desperate look was starting to make me feel bad for attempting to come between them. If this was really their happily ever after, who was I to stop it? Even if I was starting to care for Ethan in a way I wasn't ready to admit, if he wanted to be with Scarlet, I could move aside enough for him to test those waters.

Ethan took in a deep breath. I could feel his hesitancy as he stood next to me. "We can probably meet for a few minutes later," he said.

Scarlet looked relieved as she nodded. "Perfect. And really, it won't take long. Plus, I'm staying at the North Pole, too. So we can just pop outside and chat."

Cue Ethan tensing once more. "You're what?"

Scarlet's expression was a tad *too* innocent as she shrugged. "What? You always said we needed to come here for the holidays someday. So I'm here." Her smile made me sick, and for a moment, I contemplated grabbing the nearby half-eaten trifle and dumping it over her head.

But then realizing that it would embarrass Ethan even more, I refrained from doing so. Instead, I resorted to glaring at her.

"Let's go," Ethan said as he leaned close, tightened his grip, and pulled me away from Scarlet. I could tell that she had more to say, but we were out of earshot before she could get the words out.

When we got to the car, Em and Porter were waiting for us, leaning against the doors and talking. They seemed inseparable, and even though Em was trying to convince me that this was just a fun relationship, I was starting to wonder if she had feelings for Porter.

I still couldn't quite figure out what his angle was. After all, he said he was rich, but I never saw him on the phone or sneaking away to work. I wanted to think that he was genuine, but who knew in this town. As much as I hated that Em's analysis of Christmasland was starting to rub off on me, I couldn't help but feel critical of every experience. Was it real? Was it fake?

The unknown made my stomach flip.

"You guys okay?" Em asked as Ethan passed by her.

He was not trying to hide his feelings. They were as apparent as the nose on his face.

"Ethan ran into someone," I whispered as we waited for him to unlock the doors. I wanted to sit in the front passenger seat, so I could be next to him, but Porter beat me to it.

So I got to sit next to Em, like we had on the way here. She leaned in closer to me. "Someone?" she asked.

I peeked over at Ethan, who looked as if he were going to strangle the steering wheel as he drove. "I think his ex-girlfriend came to visit."

When Em didn't respond, I glanced over to see that her lips were pinched as she tried to fight a smile. I narrowed my eyes. "What?"

"Nothing," she said, shaking her head.

It wasn't nothing. I had a sinking suspicion that I knew why she was smiling. Her tagline response to everything since we got here was *"It's starting."* But I wanted to believe that Ethan was actually affected by this and not just creating an experience for me to go through.

That would be completely unfair to me. Especially since I was beginning to care for him.

Only a jerk would manipulate me like that.

For once, I wanted to believe that at least one man cared enough about me to treat me well. That at least one man wouldn't be the jerk that I feared he would be.

Ethan was different.

At least, that was what I was going to tell myself until he gave me a reason to believe otherwise.

15

ETHAN

Christmasland

I drove in silence back to the North Pole. Thankfully, Porter was distracted by some game on his phone, and Bea and Emilia were whispering in the back seat. I glanced back in the rearview mirror a few times, trying to figure out what they were talking about. But they didn't speak loud enough for me to overhear, and there was no way I could read their lips when their heads were tipped together.

So I was left with my own thoughts and feelings about my first interaction with Scarlet after our breakup.

And it wasn't good.

My stomach churned every time I thought about how I stood there, stunned. Thankfully, Bea was there to make up for my loser reaction. She picked up my slack, and I owed her a debt of gratitude.

To top it off, she helped me save face by telling Scarlet that she was my girlfriend. That wasn't what I wanted, but it did help lessen the sting I felt from standing there looking like a complete loser.

After all, I was just a glorified maid for a bed and breakfast run by my mom. There was no dignity in that. I'd wanted to have my feet under me the next time I saw Scarlet. But I felt as if I were drowning, and I was far from having any grasp on my life. And Scarlet knew it. I could see it in her gaze as she stared at me with pity.

I pulled into the back parking lot at the inn and turned off the engine. I sat there with my hands on my lap, staring forward. Porter didn't seem to notice my duress as he climbed out of the car. I thought I heard Bea whisper something to Emilia, and a moment later, they both climbed out of the car.

I wanted to stop Bea. I wanted her here with me. She helped me feel calm and collected, and I needed that now more than ever. But if she wanted to leave, I couldn't blame her. After all, I came with a lot of baggage, and I didn't want to force any of that on her.

I sighed as I gripped the steering wheel and rested my forehead on my hands. I was being a baby, I knew that, but I hadn't been prepared. The last thing I'd expected was for Scarlet to actually fly to Vermont to see me. Every time I mentioned Christmasland in the past, she just wrinkled her nose and changed the subject. The only reason she'd actually come here was because she wanted something bad. And I feared that that something was me.

The passenger door opened. I tipped my head to see Bea plopping down on the seat next to me. Her eyebrows were knit together. She turned so that she was facing me.

I could feel her stare, so I sighed and straightened. "What's up?" I asked and then cringed. I was not the kind of person who said, *what's up*. She was definitely going to be able to tell that something was wrong.

Bea narrowed her eyes. "Who is Scarlet?"

I fiddled with the steering wheel. I didn't want to relive my past—especially not with a girl that I was beginning to like as much as Bea. I wanted to be this strong, resilient person for her. But instead, I was weak and folding in on myself after a mere conversation with my ex.

Knowing that it was best to speak, I took in a deep breath. "Scarlet was my boss..." I closed my eyes for a second. "And my girlfriend." The last statement came out a whisper.

When Bea didn't respond, I glanced over to see her studying me. She didn't look disappointed or upset. If anything, she looked more resolute than ever. And that reaction confused me.

"So why is she here?"

I shrugged.

"You really don't know?" Bea didn't sound convinced. In fact, when she asked the question, it didn't seem as if she actually needed the answer. She sounded as if she already knew why Scarlet was here—just like I did.

"She wants to get back together with me."

Bea nodded and shot a finger gun at me. "Bingo." Then she grew serious. "Is that something you want as well?"

"To get back together with her?"

Bea's cheeks hinted pink, and for a moment, I wondered what that was about. Then I pushed that thought from my mind. It was probably nothing.

I shook my head. The truth was, no, I didn't want to have anything to do with Scarlet. In fact, if I never saw her again, it would be too soon. "No, I don't," I said softly.

A soft smile played on Bea's lips as she leaned in. "Then what should we do about her?"

She had a playful look in her eyes, and I wanted to be able to understand what she meant, but I was struggling. What *could* we do about it?

She reached out and patted my arm. "We already told her that we were dating, so let's really lean into it. Show her that we are happy and having the time of our lives here. She'll be jealous and want to leave." Bea raised her hand. "I swear."

I didn't allow myself to think through the logistics of what she was proposing. All I could focus on was the last bit. I would like to see Scarlet jealous and leaving. It would feel vindicating after I'd walked in on her with another man.

"You would do that for me?" I asked. The more time I spent around Bea, the harder it was for me. I liked her—I liked her a lot. And the fact that she was willing to put on a charade with me to get Scarlet to leave? Well, that just endeared her to me even more.

"Of course." Bea sighed. "I've had my share of broken hearts and disappointments. If I can help a broken-hearted friend from feeling the same, then I'll make that sacrifice."

I inwardly winced at her use of the word *friend*. I didn't want to just be her friend. I wanted her to see me as something more. But that shouldn't be what I focused on right now. My main goal was to get Scarlet out of Christmasland and out of my life, so I could focus on giving Bea the best Christmas imaginable.

I still had a half-full bingo card to check off. The sooner Scarlet packed up and left, the sooner I could get back to my time with Bea.

And I was looking forward to that time more than ever.

Feeling better about things, I opened the driver's door and climbed out. Bea waited by the car for me and then we walked side by side toward the inn. The sound of a car pulling into the driveway drew my gaze, but I was suddenly distracted by the feeling of Bea's hand slipping into my own. She threaded her fingers through mine and stepped in closer.

I glanced down, and she must have seen the startled look in my eyes. Her cheeks flushed, but she didn't move to pull her hand away. "Scarlet," she whispered as she tipped her head in the direction of the idling car.

My heart was pounding, but I managed to keep a cool head as we walked across the yard and up the front steps of the inn. Just before we slipped into the house, I glanced behind me to see that Scarlet had gotten out of her car and was standing in the parking lot, watching us.

I hated the rush of guilt that came from seeing her stand there with her eyebrows knit together in confusion. I wanted to go out and explain myself, but I knew that would only open me up to disappointment. So I turned my focus forward and followed Bea.

Once we were inside, I stopped as Mom stared at the two of us. She was standing behind the receptionist desk with her readers perched on her nose and her hand midway through turning the page of the book in front of her. Her gaze moved from our faces down to our hands.

I quickly dropped my hand. But Bea didn't seem as desperate to step away from me. Instead, she remained calm as she slipped off her jacket and brought the bouquet of flowers and gift cards over to Mom.

"I won," she declared.

That seemed to be distraction enough. Mom cheered as she rounded the desk and pulled Bea into a hug. "You did?" she asked as she pulled back.

Bea nodded. "It's a Christmas miracle. I got the grand prize."

Mom wrapped her arm around Bea's shoulders and led her into the dining room. I hung up my jacket and followed after them. There was no way I wanted to be left alone when Scarlet came into the inn. I was ready to put some distance between me and the front door.

Mom was telling Bea that she'd tasted the cookies after we left and knew right away that they were going to be a winner. Then she instructed us to eat lunch. Just before she left to greet Scarlet, she hovered next to me.

"We need to talk later," she said under her breath.

I couldn't agree more, but this was not the time or place. Once Scarlet was settled in her room and Bea was distracted, Mom and I had a lot of things to talk about.

Lunch was cranberry and turkey sandwiches. Mom even sliced and fried the potatoes to make her special rosemary chips. The salty chips tasted amazing after the amount of sugar I'd had. We sat at the farthest table from the foyer and ate.

Bea kept the conversation light after Emilia and Porter joined us with their own plates of food. They talked about the plans for the rest of the day, and I only half listened. I was distracted by watching Mom talk to Scarlet. Once they disappeared upstairs, with Scarlet's suitcases in hand, I felt as if I could relax.

When I turned my attention back to the people sitting next to me, I noticed them all watching me with an intent look. I glanced between them. Was I supposed to talk?

"So are you going?" Emilia asked after she took a sip of her apple cider.

"Going?" I picked up my half-eaten sandwich and took a big bite.

Emilia nodded. "Tomorrow. Are you going?"

I glanced from Emilia to Bea and then over to Porter. They all looked as if they knew what was going on; I was the only one in the dark.

"Yes?" I finally said, hoping that was the right answer.

"You are?" Porter asked. The surprise in his voice had me instantly regretting my response.

But when Bea reached over and patted my hand, she helped me feel better. "See. I told you. It's for a couple, but we'll have fun with it."

What in the world did I just agree to?

"Snowtop looks pretty romantic," Emilia said as she slipped a chip into her mouth. "I mean, there's a romantic dinner, a midnight sleigh ride, cuddling by the fire..." Her voice trailed off, and I noticed that her gaze was focused on Bea as if she expected that was all it would take to convince her friend not to go.

Finally feeling caught up on the conversation, I sipped my water and shrugged. "We can make it work, right? It'll be fun." I gave Bea a smile, and her expression perked in response.

She nodded resolutely as she turned her focus back to Emilia. "Yeah. It'll be great."

Emilia didn't look convinced but didn't push it. Instead, she focused her attention on Porter, and they started brainstorming what they were going to do. I took this time to peek down at Bea. She was picking at her sandwich. So I bumped her with my shoulder.

"Are you sure?" I asked.

Bea glanced up at me. "About what?"

I nodded to the gift cards that were resting on the table next to the flowers. "About taking me. You should take Emilia. I'm sure she'd enjoy it."

Bea paused and studied Emilia before she shook her head. "Nah. She wants to spend some time with Porter. Besides, I can't leave you here by yourself for the day." She leaned forward. "Not with Scrooge upstairs."

I snorted at her description of Scarlet. It was quite accurate.

After we finished lunch, Bea and Emilia said that they were heading to their room to relax for a bit. I waited until they disappeared upstairs before I headed into the kitchen to rinse our dishes and load them in the dishwasher. Porter stayed in the living room, where he picked up a book to read.

I was alone as I stepped up to the sink and turned on the faucet. I waited for the water to warm before I started rinsing each dish. My mind started to wander. Surprisingly, it steered clear of Scarlet. Instead, the only face that kept drifting into my mind was Bea's. Her smile. The way she looked up at me. The expression on her face when she won. All of it seemed cemented in my mind.

"Feeling okay?"

Mom's voice startled me enough that I dropped the plate I was rinsing. It clattered in the sink but thankfully didn't break. I turned to see Mom standing next to me, peering into the sink after the dish as well.

"What?" I asked as I forced my heart rate to return to normal and finished loading the plate into the dishwasher.

Mom poured herself a mug of coffee. "I was wondering if you

were feeling okay. I mean, I did just see you walk into the inn holding Beatrice's hand." She peered over the rim of her mug at me as she took a sip. "What was that about?"

I cleared my throat. "I don't know what you are talking about." I picked up a glass to rinse.

Mom reached over and took it from me. She set it on the counter and turned off the water. I sighed. She wasn't going to let this go, so I turned my focus on her. "What?"

Mom pursed her lips. I cleared my throat and offered her an apologetic smile. "What?" I asked, softer this time.

Mom studied me for a moment before she sighed. "What is your game plan, Ethan? I mean, I know we talked about giving Beatrice a Christmas to remember, but is that what you are doing?"

I turned my focus back out the window and rested my hands near the sink. I took in a deep breath. What did I want to do? I knew that having Bea help me save face in front of Scarlet was honorable enough. After all, it was her idea.

But was I just taking advantage of her? That wasn't what I wanted to do. I'd been so focused on how I was feeling over these last few hours that I hadn't thought about what this might to do Bea.

Was I going to hurt her in the end? I didn't want to.

"I would suggest that if you don't know what you are doing, perhaps you pull away?" Mom was fiddling with the handle of her mug when I turned my attention back to her.

That wasn't fair. She'd convinced me to play along, and now she was telling me to back away? Realizing that Mom needed more context, I turned to face her.

"Bea is just helping me." I blew out my breath. "Scarlet showed up and wants to talk. Bea saw her and helped interject on my behalf." I grabbed the next dish and flipped on the faucet. "That's it. Nothing more."

"Scarlet?" Mom asked.

I nodded as I stared at the water. "Yes. She flew in all the way from Chicago. You just checked her in."

"Really?" Mom's voice was a whisper.

I rinsed the dish and then stuck it in the dishwasher. "So it's all fake. All of it." It was strange, but saying those words hurt. It felt as if a dagger had been shoved into my heart. All of my experiences with Bea were fake. What I'd planned for her and what she'd proposed to me. None of it had to do with either of us wanting to be in a relationship. Instead, we were just creating a facade for the other.

Or, at least, she was creating that for me. The more time I spent with Bea, the more time I wanted to spend with her. I liked being around her. She made me laugh. She was easy to talk to. If planning ridiculous Christmas activities kept her around me, then I would keep doing that.

But for Bea, our "relationship" was nothing more than a smoke screen to help me save face in front of Scarlet. And even if we were successful in dispelling her, I was still going to be left alone in the end.

Bea would finish up her vacation here and leave. While I would be stuck behind with no future and only memories of the past.

And that sucked. All of it.

"Are you sure you're okay with pretending?" Mom finally asked.

I swallowed hard against the lump in my throat. The truth was, no, I wasn't okay with pretending. I was tired of this whole charade. I wanted something real, but when I lived in a town that literally peddled in fake realities, it was hard to remember what that even felt like.

So instead of speaking the truth, I lied for the umpteenth time since coming home. I nodded and shrugged. "Yep. I'll be fine."

Mom didn't look convinced but thankfully didn't push me further. Instead she just nodded and moved to pull some butter from the fridge. We worked in silence, her prepping the kitchen to make cookies and me loading the dishwasher. Once I was done, I excused myself and disappeared to my room. Thankfully Porter hadn't decided to do the same.

I needed some privacy. I needed a break to gather my thoughts and focus. If I was going to pretend, then I needed to stop caring. But I feared that no matter how many times I tried to convince myself of that, it was going to be difficult.

Because I cared.

A little too much.

16

BEATRICE

I was sprawled out on the bed, watching Em as she attempted to break down what I'd just told her. She was tapping her chin and casting her gaze upwards as she worked through my predicament in her mind.

When we'd got back to the room, I told her everything. I told her about the food fight, the almost kiss, and my agreement to be Ethan's fake girlfriend as he tried to save face in front of his ex. Em's eyes got wider and wider as I spoke. She had not been anticipating it, and when I was finished, I'd shocked my best friend into complete silence.

She took in a deep breath and returned her gaze to me. "Well, how do you feel about this?" she asked.

I chewed my bottom lip. I honestly hated that question. I felt a mess. My insides were jumbled, and my brain was of no help either. I wanted someone else to tell me what to do—what to think. I didn't want to weed through my feelings and come up with a logical, well-thought-out plan to victory.

I groaned as I grabbed a nearby pillow and pulled it over my face. I held it tight as I kicked my feet in the air. After a few seconds, I removed it and glanced over at her. Em looked unimpressed. "Feel better?"

I squeezed my eyes closed and shook my head. "No."

The bed moved as Em lay down next to me. I glanced over at her and saw that she was studying the ceiling above us. It was strange, seeing Em so stoic. Her normal come-what-may attitude was gone, and she looked more mature as she stared above her.

"Did I break you?" I asked.

Em laughed. "No, you didn't break me." She sighed. "I'm worried I broke you."

I furrowed my brow. "What does that mean? Why would you think you broke me?"

Em tipped her head to study me. "I dragged you here. I convinced you that everything was part of the story. I don't want you to be hurt."

My chest tightened at her words. "Hurt? Why would I get hurt?" As soon as the words left my lips, I wanted to take them back. I knew what she was saying. She feared what I feared.

That Ethan was just playing a part and that none of this was real.

"Oh," I said. The emotions in my throat made my voice become a whisper. I didn't realize how soul-crushing it would be to hear that my best friend also feared what I had kept inside this entire trip. I guess I figured that if Em never confirmed it, that idea just might remain in my head where it belonged.

But now that she admitted that she felt that way too, I was left with nothing but the reality of my situation.

"So what do I do?" Why had I allowed myself to become an idiot? Everyone else in Christmasland understood the façade. Why couldn't I get on board?

Em sighed and shifted so that she was on her side. She studied me as she drew circles on the comforter with her finger. "Do you want to leave?"

I both loved and hated the fact that she was offering this. It was a testament to our friendship that she was willing to give up something she loved for me, and I appreciated that. But there was no way I was going to become that kind of friend. I was the one who read into this place too much. I was the one who'd let myself care.

And even if I believed, deep down, there might be a chance that Ethan actually cared for me, I needed to get my head on straight and lock my heart in my chest where it belonged. Plus, it was a joke that I would actually find love in a place like Christmasland. Every relationship I'd had in one of the biggest cities in the world ended in heartbreak, why did I think I would find something different in a small town like this?

No. This was a test for me, and I was failing. I was going to get up, get dressed, and enjoy myself. If Ethan was playing a game, then I was going to play too.

I could do this. I could.

We spent the next fifteen minutes getting ready. I had to convince Em a few times that I'd be fine, especially when she gave me the pursed lips and raised eyebrow look. I knew she was asking me if I was okay.

Even if I wasn't sure I was, that didn't matter. I was here for her. I was going to give her the best Christmas experience because I knew she cared about it.

"What do you want to do?" I asked as I leaned against the doorframe and watched her lace up her boots.

She paused as she glanced up at me. "What do I want to do?"

I nodded. "What would make this the quintessential Christmas for you?"

Em finished tying her lace and stood. "The quintessential Christmas?"

This was a fun conversation. Her repeating everything I said. "Yes."

A slow smile emerged on her lips. "Are you coming around to Christmas?"

I nudged her with my shoulder. "I've always loved Christmas."

She gave me a look that said, *yeah right.*

I laughed as she locked our door. "Okay, so maybe I don't love it as much as you do. But I enjoy the idea of Christmas." I raised my hand and left a small space between my thumb and forefinger. "Just on a smaller scale than you."

Em linked arms with me as we made our way to the stairs. "I really want to decorate a tree," she said.

I thought about her request as we descended each step. "A tree?"

She nodded. "I love stringing lights. Stringing popcorn. Putting on ornaments." She sighed as we paused on the last step. "It was something I used to do with my grandparents before they passed."

A familiar ache rose up inside of me, but I pushed it down. This wasn't the time or the place to revel in my missed childhood experiences. If anything, it was time to take this holiday by the horns and experience it like it was meant to be experienced.

"Let's do it, then," I said, probably a bit too loud.

Carol appeared from around the corner. She was holding a tray of chocolate goodies in one hand and had an intrigued expression on her face. "What are we doing this late afternoon, ladies?" Her smile was wide. She looked like she was forcing her enthusiasm, and it made me wonder what was going on.

"Everything okay?" I asked as I stepped forward.

Carol's lips tightened, and her eyes looked as if they were glistening. Like she was on the verge of tears. Concerned that something bad had happened, I reached out and took the tray from her. "Come sit down," I instructed as I nodded toward a nearby dining room chair.

She didn't fight me. Instead, she sat while I put the tray on the nearby credenza. When I returned, Carol was dabbing her eyes with a holiday-print handkerchief, and Em was patting her shoulder in a rhythmic way.

I knelt down in front of her and waited for her to finish. When she was done, she cradled her hands in her lap and smiled down at me.

"Forgive this old woman. I just get emotional this time of year." She sniffled. "I was just thinking about you and how the holidays must have been." She reached down and grabbed my hand. She brought it up to her lap and started patting it. "I want to give you the best Christmas ever."

I studied her. Even though I was certain I was never going to love this holiday as much as she did, I did appreciate her desire to make this Christmas a memorable one for me.

"The good news is the bar for me is set pretty low. I mean, I've already experienced more Christmas festivities here than I ever have before." I reached out and patted her hand that had stilled on top of mine. "You're doing a good job. I'm loving my time here so far."

It was strange that she was focused in on me this much. After all, she did have an inn full of guests. But there was something about Em and I that had her undivided attention. Or perhaps she did this for every guest. Who was I to know?

She smiled, her normal relaxed and cheerful smile, and then nodded. "I'm so happy to hear that." Then she glanced from Em back to me. "What can I do to make your stay even better?"

This was the perfect opportunity. Requesting a tree would satisfy Em and help Carol feel better about my stay here. "Em was telling me how much she missed decorating a Christmas tree this year. Maybe we can arrange something this evening?" I knew that with a tree in every room, she might not have space for one more, but when her smile widened, I knew it was not going to be a problem.

She nodded fervently and stood. "Yes. That is a fabulous idea." Then she hurried from the room.

I straightened at the same time that Em stood. She glanced over at me. "What was that about?"

I shrugged, but before I could respond, Carol appeared again, this time dragging Ethan behind her. My heart picked up speed at the sight of him. He looked as if he'd just woken up and was disoriented. When his gaze landed on me, he smiled briefly before he turned his focus back to his mom.

"What do you need?" he asked as he pushed his hand through his hair once she stopped in front of us.

"You need to take these girls out to pick a tree." She waved back and forth from Em to me. "They need to decorate a Christmas tree."

I raised my hand. "It's really no big deal. I mean, if you have a small one, we'd be happy to use that one."

I could feel Ethan's gaze on me. My cheeks flushed as I forced myself to keep my attention on Carol and not slip into the insanity that came from focusing on Ethan.

Carol waved away my comment. "Nonsense. He can take you to the farm, and you can chop one down." She linked arms with Em and me and started guiding us toward the door. "I planted those trees a few years ago. They are ready to come down." Once we were at the coat rack, she dropped our arms and located our jackets.

"If you leave now, it'll still be light out, and you'll be back in time for dinner." She leaned in. "I'm making a turkey with gravy. You won't want to miss it."

I begged to differ. My pants were already starting to feel a tad tight from all the goodness she fed us. But I didn't have time to resist as my jacket was shoved into my hands. I slipped it on as Carol instructed Ethan to get ready as well.

Porter popped in from the living room, which caused Em to perk up. He got his shoes and jacket on, and then the two of them headed out to the porch to wait for us. I gave Ethan a sheepish smile. I was fiddling with the zipper on my jacket. I didn't want to seem like I was waiting for him...even if I kind of was.

I wanted to make sure he was okay with this. After all, the

expression on his face was a sour one. He looked as if he were struggling with something, and I wasn't sure if it was because of me or the sudden appearance of his ex-girlfriend.

"You okay?" I asked as I leaned in with a soft smile. I wanted to show him that I was not a threat.

He zipped up his jacket and plopped a hat on his head. "Yeah. Great." Then he frowned. "Why?"

I shrugged. I could tell that he was lying to me, but I wasn't sure if I should push him further or if I even wanted to know why he felt he needed to lie. And really, was it my place? After all, I was just a guest here. At some point, I was going to need to leave and return to the normal world.

Perhaps, he'd just realized that as well.

What was the point of starting a real relationship if the other one was destined to leave? He was being wise, and I should follow suit.

"Nothing. Just checking," I said as I shrugged and pulled my gloves from my jacket pocket.

Ethan didn't say anything more. Instead he gave me a curt nod and then headed out the front door to join Em and Porter.

Still confused, I decided to push that confusion from my mind and focus on the present and what we were doing. I was here to enjoy myself, and I was going to do that. I was going to forget my frustration over Ethan and experience Christmas like Em and Carol wanted for me.

I could worry about what Ethan's reactions meant later.

For now, I was going to be the jolliest guest in Christmasland ever.

After all, what other choice did I have?

If I was going to stay here, I was going to enjoy myself.

No matter what.

17

ETHAN

I sighed as I pulled up to the Christmas tree farm that Mom had started years ago. I let the inn's truck idle for a moment before I turned the key and declared, "We're here."

Emilia squealed and opened the door. I peeked back at Bea, who was smiling just as big, as she opened her door and climbed out. Porter seemed to be enjoying himself, too. He and Emilia had really hit it off, and despite the fact that he was blatantly lying to the girl, he didn't seem to feel any guilt over it.

Not like me.

No matter how much I tried to convince myself that it didn't matter, that it was okay that I was pretending for Bea, I couldn't shake the guilty feeling inside of me. I was a fraud. I was—in a way—being as untruthful to her as Scarlet had been to me.

Even though with Scarlet, we'd been together and pledged our fidelity to each other. I couldn't draw that line of distinction in my own mind.

I wasn't being honest with Bea, period, and no matter how hard I tried to justify it, nothing made me feel better.

I looked out through the windshield. Em and Porter were talking, and Bea was watching me. She'd picked up on my hesitation—which I hated—and I could tell that she was concerned. I was trying to not let it bother me, but I was failing. So much so that when Mom saw my reaction after she proposed the tree chopping idea, she gave me a stern look and told me to stop focusing on what I couldn't control and focus on what I could.

So that is why I got out of bed and forced myself to participate.

Pushing the thoughts of worry from my mind, I opened the door and stepped out as Tyler walked up to us. He ran the tree farm for Mom, and when he saw me, he headed in my direction.

"Carol need another tree?" he asked in a laughing tone.

I nodded. "Yes and no. She wants us to get a tree for our guests to decorate." I motioned toward Bea and Emilia. They gave him a smile, and he introduced himself. After the pleasantries were over, he motioned for us to follow.

"We've got some good ones further out. No one has seemed to want to go that far, but if you're willing to take the time, I guarantee that they are worth it."

Emilia squealed, and from her reaction I could tell that was exactly what we were going to do. Tyler handed over the keys to two four-wheelers and made a joke about using an axe or a chainsaw.

Right when I was about to take him up on the chainsaw offer, Emilia piped up. "Let's use an axe."

I turned my attention to her. She must not know the kind of effort it took to chop down a tree with an axe. But when I saw Bea nod, I knew there was no way I could change their minds. So I leaned toward Tyler and requested an axe.

He gave me a laughing look as he headed into the small shed and emerged with an axe over his shoulder. "Have fun with this," he said as he handed it to me.

I pursed my lips and nodded. "Yep."

We headed over to the four-wheelers. I threw a set of keys to Porter, who caught them, then I turned to Bea. "Ready?" I asked as

I dropped the axe into the trailer that was attached to the four-wheeler. Then I swung my leg over the seat and shoved the keys into the ignition.

"I'm getting on that?" she asked as she pointed toward it.

I nodded. "It's the only way we are going to be able to get the tree back." I tried to convince myself that she was hesitant because machines like this could be dangerous, not because she didn't want to ride with me. So, I just offered her a smile as I studied her.

She chewed her lip, and I could see the inner war going on inside of her. Porter and Emilia were already on the other four-wheeler, and Porter turned the key, which caused the engine to roar to life.

"It'll be okay," I said as I leaned forward to catch Bea's gaze. "I'll keep you safe."

Bea glanced from me to the seat behind me and then sighed. "Promise?"

I nodded as I handed her a helmet. "I swear my life on it."

She hesitated but then took the helmet from me and slipped it on. "I'm trusting you," she said, her voice muffled.

That statement felt like a dagger to my heart. I wanted to tell her not to get on the four-wheeler. I wanted to take her home and leave this place forever. I knew she just meant that she trusted my driving, but I couldn't help but extrapolate her words to other aspects of our relationship.

How could I have been so deceitful to her? I'd purposely conspired with my mom, and I couldn't help but feel like everything we had done since only added to the conspiracy. Everything about Christmasland was part of this charade of the perfect Christmas town.

Yet, we all knew it was a lie. A lie that I allowed myself to keep telling Bea.

I shook my head slightly to clear it as Bea climbed on behind me. She wrapped her arms around my waist and pulled herself close. My entire body reacted to her nearness. I wanted to pull away and lean in at the same time. There hadn't been many times in my life where I'd felt this conflicted, and I could normally walk away when presented with the choice.

But not this time. Not with Bea.

"Ready?" I asked as my hand hovered over the key. I needed to get out of my head and focus on what we were here to do. Get a tree and get back to the inn.

Bea nodded, and I could feel the movement as her head rested on my back. I gave Porter a thumbs-up and started the engine. We took off down the cleared path toward the place that Tyler had recommended. The sun was on top of the trees, reflecting off of the snow. In an hour, it would be behind the trees as the evening arrived. The desire not to be out here in darkness came over me, so I sped up.

It only took about fifteen minutes to reach the far end of Mom's tree farm. We'd passed by many different ages of trees, from tiny to teenager. I pulled up to the large, adult trees that were hidden in the back and turned off the engine.

Bea slipped off, and I followed after her.

Emilia was already off and removing her helmet when we approached. "It's beautiful here," she said. Her cheeks were flushed, and her eyes sparkled as she glanced around.

She wasn't lying. There was a certain calm in the forest. The natural woods resided on the outskirts of the farm, giving a secluded and enclosed feeling. And when I breathed in, the smell of clean air and pine filled my nose. It had a calming effect on me, which I needed.

I stood there as Emilia and Bea whispered to each other. I could tell that they were assessing the trees that surrounded us. When they finally zeroed in on one, they nodded and then motioned for us to meet up with them. I grabbed the axe and headed in their direction.

"This is the one," Bea said, her voice breathy with a hint of reverence. I scanned over the tree, wincing as my gaze landed on the trunk. It was about the size of my thigh. This was going to be fun to chop.

"This one?" I asked and then glanced over at Porter. "Wanna take this?" I bumped the axe that was resting on my shoulder and nodded toward it.

Porter scoffed. "Nah, man. This is all you," he said as he took a step back.

A disappointed look flashed over Emilia's face as she watched Porter take a step back. It was strange, but it almost seemed as if she'd *wanted* Porter to take on the task. I sighed as I turned my focus back to the tree. Well, it wasn't going to chop itself. We were already here, so we might as well return with something.

I kicked away the snow at the base of the trunk and began chopping. I wanted the tree to fall away from us, so I focused on chopping out a wedge from the trunk. I could hear Emilia cheer with every blow I landed. I wondered if Bea felt the same.

I took a moment while I wiggled the axe from the trunk and glanced in their direction. Emilia was gripping onto Bea's arm, and her cheeks were flushed as she bounced up and down. Bea looked as if she were trying to counteract her friend's reaction by remaining stoic.

I was a little disappointed when I turned my attention back to the tree. It sounded lame in my head, but I kind of wanted Bea to be just as enthusiastic as Emilia was. Well, maybe not *just* as enthusiastic, but even just a little bit would be nice. It would at least make all of this work worth it.

The tree started to sway from the blows, and I focused my attention on what I was doing. A few seconds passed, and I realized that there was no stopping the movement now. It was coming down.

"Timber!" I yelled as I stepped back and watched the remaining intact bark begin to bend. The tree tipped and landed with a *poof* onto the snow behind it. Emilia cheered, and my heart surged when I saw Bea's smile emerge. This was the kind of reaction I'd been hoping for.

"This is so exciting," Emilia said as she hurried over to the tree and stared reverently down at it.

I chuckled and turned my efforts to the intact tree bark as I hacked away at it. "You're easy to please," I teased.

Emilia sighed. "When it comes to Christmas, I have a hard time not finding joy in the little things."

Once the tree was fully detached, I swung the axe over my shoulder and reached down to grab one of the low-hanging branches. Once it was firmly in my hand, I turned to see Bea standing right behind me.

"Whoa," I said as I stepped back.

Bea shot me an embarrassed look. "I was wondering if you wanted me to carry that," she said as she nodded toward the axe.

I glanced at it and then back to her. "Um, sure."

I swung it to the ground and then handed it to Bea. She grabbed the handle, her fingers brushing against mine in the process. Even though we both wore gloves, the pressure from her fingers to mine caused my heart to start beating hard.

Worried that she might hear my heart racing, I cleared my throat and began to drag the tree through the snow and over to the trailer. Emilia was chatting away with Porter as they followed after us.

I kept my focus on loading the tree and getting us out of here. I was tired of being so distracted by Bea, and I knew that some distance between us would be beneficial. This whole charade was beginning to wear on me, and if I didn't start facing reality soon, I was going to lose my grip on it.

We loaded everything back up and climbed onto the four-wheelers. Bea seemed less hesitant when she slipped onto the seat behind me. How quickly she wrapped her arms around me and held me tight shocked me. She was getting more and more comfortable around me.

Which only made me feel worse.

I was the jerk who was leading her on. I was the jerk that she was trying to protect from his ex-girlfriend. She came here for a relaxing vacation, and I hijacked it in more ways than one.

We rode in silence back to the parking lot. Even though we didn't talk, there was a whole lot going on in my head as I drove down the path. There was so much that I wanted to say. So much that I wanted to admit to. But I couldn't find it in myself to say any of it.

If I told her that her experiences in Christmasland were fabricated, would she doubt that I'd created them with sincerity? Would I be able to tell her that, no matter how events happened, I was starting to care for her?

Would she be able to trust me?

As I turned off the engine and climbed off the four-wheeler, I was beginning to realize that, no, she wouldn't be able to forgive me. And that was assuming she cared about me in the first place. Which just may be me manifesting what I actually wanted to happen.

And if she didn't care about me, I was only exposing myself to more pain. I wasn't sure my heart could handle another blow. Scarlet damaged me more than I cared to admit, and if I put myself out there just to have Bea back down, I was going to break that much more.

The more I thought about it, the faster I began to realize that all I needed to do was get through the rest of this holiday season. If I backed away and closed myself off to the potential pain that I knew was coming my way, I would stay safe.

Caring about someone only led to more damage.

If I wanted to protect myself, then I needed to stay away from Bea.

Far, far away.

BEATRICE

Ethan was quiet...too quiet.

The whole drive back to the inn was silent as he sat in the driver's seat with his gaze focused on the road and his wrist resting on the steering wheel. I could tell something was bothering him—the way he was working his jaw muscles even though he wasn't eating anything was a dead giveaway.

I wanted to ask him what was wrong, but I wasn't sure how to do it so that Em and Porter didn't hear. I figured they might not even pay attention, as they were currently swapping childhood Christmas stories in the back, but I decided not to risk it.

I was going to ask him when we got back to the inn, and I could pull him aside.

Once he pulled into the parking spot in the back, we all climbed out. The sun was now snuggled just above the horizon, casting its last rays of light through the trees and across the snow around us. I pulled my jacket closer to my body as the wind whipped around me.

I lingered around the truck while Porter and Ethan unstrapped the tree and slid it out of the bed and onto the ground. Ethan told Porter that he had it from here, and Em and

Porter hurried to the front of the inn and disappeared. I wasn't in any rush, so I stood behind Ethan and waited for him to move.

He grabbed onto the bottom branch and began dragging the tree across the driveway. He made a point of sticking to the unpacked snow, which I figured would do less damage to the tree as he pulled it.

I hurried to fall into step with him. Not wanting to discover how he felt about me waiting for him, I kept my gaze downturned to the snow beneath my feet.

"I've got this." His voice was low and masked. I couldn't tell if he was attempting to hide his emotions, or if he just felt platonic toward me.

As much as I wanted to believe it was the former, I couldn't help but think that, perhaps, I'd misread everything that had happened between us. I'd awoken this morning thinking that we were heading down the path toward friendship—or even more— but I was beginning to think that was a pipe dream.

That there was no way I should have read his actions toward me as anything other than him being nice to a guest.

"I can help," I said as I hurried to the other side of the tree and grabbed hold of a branch on that side.

Ethan grunted in protest but didn't say anything. Instead, he kept his focus on the inn as he dragged the tree toward it.

That was a decent sign. He wasn't so annoyed by me that he was asking me to leave. I could take some solace in that. Just as we reached the porch, I stopped. Effectively stopping him as well. He glanced over at me with his brows furrowed.

"You okay?" he asked.

The was a hint of concern to his voice that only made me angrier. If he cared—like I suspected he did—why did it feel like we were constantly in this dance of one step forward, two steps back?

What was so wrong with me that he couldn't just admit how he felt—if he felt it. Was it that hard to imagine a future with me? The least he could do was fake it. After all, in every Hallmark movie I'd ever seen, even the villain pretended to like the hero at one point.

"Are you okay?" I asked and then realized how dumb that response was. Way to answer a question…with the exact same question.

Ethan paused and studied me. I could tell he was assessing what to say next, but I wasn't sure what he was going to say. I kept my gaze focused on him. If he was going to retreat from me, I was going to make sure he knew I was watching him.

"I'm fine," he finally said after he blew out his breath. "I'm just cold and ready to get this tree into the house." He nodded toward the door.

I studied him for a few seconds longer before I sighed and nodded. There was no way I believed him, but what else could I do? If I confronted him, I was going to be exposed as the loser I felt I was. And I was tired of feeling so broken all the time. Being a single woman did take its toll on me when I let it. I couldn't help but feel everyone's wonderment when they discovered that I was not, nor had ever been, married.

It was as if I were some sort of social leper.

Not wanting to wear my emotions out on my sleeve in sub-zero temperatures, I nodded and started moving again. If he wasn't going to open up, what was the sense in me trying?

When we got inside, we stomped the snow off our shoes. It took a few of us to lift the tree and bring it inside. We tipped it against the far wall while we removed our jackets, gloves, and hats. Carol moved around the tree, oohing and aahing at how perfect it was.

"Tyler doesn't disappoint," she said as she stood in front of us with her hands on her hips, her cheeks glowing with appreciation. I just gave her a smile and nodded.

"Tyler didn't pick this," Ethan said as he pushed his hands

through his hair. It had flattened from his hat. "He told us to go to the edge of the property and cut it down ourselves."

Carol hurried over to him and patted his shoulder. "Oh, you big baby. It's the things you have to work the hardest for that make all the pain worth it."

I couldn't help but feel as if her statement was directed toward me. The way she was staring at me made me shiver. Did she know something that I didn't?

"So where are we going to set this?" Em asked as she clapped her hands and rubbed them together like she'd just asked something sinister.

Carol perked up as she moved away from Ethan and waved for us to follow her into the living room. A spot had been cleared right by the fireplace. "I was thinking here," she said as she stood in the spot and raised her arms like she was pretending to be a tree.

"By the fire?" Ethan asked.

I turned to see that he had followed us but was keeping his distance. He was leaning his shoulder against the doorframe.

Carol tsked him. "It'll be fine. We'll keep it far enough away that there's no chance of a fire." She waved away his comment. "Now, who wants to go to the barn and get out the ornaments?"

Em and Porter raised their hands, and before anyone could join them, they had their jackets in hand and were heading out the door. I gave Em an inquisitive look, to which she just giggled and waved me away.

At least she was having fun.

"That leaves you two to get the tree in the stand." Carol waved toward the green tree stand in the corner. "I found this in the basement. It should work perfectly with the tree."

I parted my lips to tell her that I was planning on joining Em and Porter, but Carol didn't wait for my response. Instead, she hurried from the room when a man lingering by the front desk called her name.

Now alone with Ethan, I turned to peek at him. His jaw was set, and he had moved his arms up to fold them across his chest. He looked irritated, and I wasn't sure how to read his response. Was he irritated at me or the fact that Carol hadn't taken him up on his suggestion to move the tree?

"It'll be okay," I said before I could stop myself.

Ethan flicked his gaze over to me, the furrow between his eyebrows deepening. "What will?"

I swallowed as I waved to the empty spot that had been earmarked for the tree. "The location."

Ethan sighed and shrugged. "Yeah, you're probably right." He pushed off the doorframe and went to grab the tree.

I hurried over to the tree stand and set it in the middle of the space before I made my way into the foyer to help him. The tree began making its way toward me. I could barely make Ethan out from behind the branches.

"Can I help?" I asked as I stepped out of the way.

"Nah, I got it." His voice was muffled, and all I could see was his arms as they wrapped around the tree.

"Really, I can help," I said as I followed after him. I reached out and brushed his arm, and he jolted back as if I'd burned him. Realizing that I'd probably startled him, I apologized.

Ethan didn't respond. He just kept moving. There was no way he was going to let me help, and I was trying hard to not let that hurt my feelings. I kept pace with him until we got to the stand. After a few failed attempts to stick the tree into the base, I finally dropped to the ground and helped him thread the needle.

Once the trunk was inside, I worked on tightening the screws so that the tree was upright and secure. Ethan joined me once the tree was stable, to tighten them past the point that I could get them, but he kept his attention on everything but me.

I tried to offer him a smile, but he never took me up on it. As soon as the tree was secure, he was out from under the tree in a flash. I blew out my breath as I stayed in my spot. Closing my eyes, I tried to push away the feelings of hurt that brewed inside of me.

I had just read into things too much, that was all. He was here as an employee of the inn, and I had been the ridiculous guest who had romanticized everything. The sooner I woke up and realized what was truly going on, the better off I would be.

It didn't take long for Em and Porter to return. They were each carrying boxes of decorations in their arms and laughing. I hurried out from under the tree and forced a smile. Ethan was halfway across the room when he stopped and turned to face them.

"Where are you going?" Porter asked as he set the boxes down next to tree.

"I was gonna—"

"Stay and help decorate." Carol finished his sentence just as she walked into the room.

Ethan stared at her and then at the tree and then back at her. He sighed and shrugged as he moved back to where he'd been brooding earlier. "I guess I'm staying to help decorate."

I wanted to tell him that there was no need. If he didn't want to be here, no one was going to force him to be here. But from the determined look on Carol's face, I began to realize that was not true. *Carol* had every intention of making him be here. Which I found funny.

A grown man bossed around by his petite mom.

Ugh. Why did that just endear him to me even more? Why wasn't I a stronger person?

We started with the lights. It was nice to have Em and Porter there to help ease the tension in the room. They were laughing and singing Christmas songs, and I found myself humming along despite the grinch in the corner. His solemn expression didn't change as he stood there, detangling lights.

I wanted him to cheer up—I just wasn't sure how.

Just as I went to grab tinsel from the box, movement in the

doorway caught my attention. Standing there, looking like a goddess in her red turtleneck dress, was Scarlet, fully living up to her name. She had one hand on her hip, and her focus was set on Ethan.

The desire to save him from her clutches rushed over me, and before I even had time to think, my bundle of tinsel and I made our way over to him. I leaned forward and pressed my lips to his cheek.

He jolted, his head whipping up and the look of death flashing in his eyes. One would have thought that I had just stabbed him with a knife or something. I thought it was quite the overreaction, but Ethan didn't calm down.

He blinked once. Twice.

"Scarlet," I whispered as I tipped my head toward where she stood. If I didn't explain myself soon, I feared he was going to have a brain aneurysm right then and there, next to the artificial reindeer that adorned the living room.

"What?" he asked. Thankfully, he had enough control over his voice that his tone came out raspy, and I was fairly confident that Scarlet did not hear him.

"Scarlet is watching," I said and then laughed.

He frowned and then tipped his head slightly to the side. He must have seen her, because suddenly, he was fake laughing right along with me.

"Why are we laughing?" he asked through his smile.

"We need to look in love," I hissed. I leaned forward and tousled his hair.

He flinched like he thought I was going to hit him, but then returned to normal.

Geez. There was nothing like a guy physically trying to get away from my touch to make a girl feel wanted.

"How long do we laugh for?" he asked.

I glowered at him. He was horrible at playing like we were in a relationship. Plus, his obvious repulsion to me just added more fuel to my anger. It was as if he couldn't imagine a relationship with me, even though I couldn't help but envision one myself.

Out of spite, and the desire not to stand there laughing anymore, I slid the lights that he was working on from his lap and plopped sideways in its place. I wrapped my arms around his neck—ignoring the tension of his body—and nuzzled my face in his neck.

"You stink at faking a relationship," I whispered in his ear.

He was frozen, but I didn't care. I was going to sit here until he pulled out the candy cane that was shoved up his bum. He needed to learn to relax.

Moments ticked by before he did anything. Right when I began to fear that I'd taken this too far, his hand wrapped around my back, and suddenly, he was pulling me closer to his chest.

I pulled back and stared at him. His gaze didn't leave mine as he held me there. I could feel his heart pounding against his chest, and I feared he could feel mine doing the same. Or perhaps, mine was hammering inside of me so hard, I was actually just feeling my own.

"Is this better?" he growled. He brought up his free hand to cradle my cheek. His gaze never wavered from mine.

Everything around me began to grow hazy as I studied him. There was a fire in his gaze that took my breath away. Was it because he wanted me? Or because he wanted Scarlet to believe that he wanted me.

"This is good," I said, taking my turn to freeze now. I wanted to move, but he had me in a trance that nothing was getting through,

It was like this was what I wanted.

His hand lingered on my cheek. His fingertips brushed my skin, causing goose bumps. I could feel myself lean into him. My gaze drifting down to his lips and then back up to hold his gaze.

For a moment, I wondered if he was going to kiss me. And in that moment, that was all that I wanted. I forgot my fear. Forgot my worry. Even if Ethan was playing me, I was okay with it. I wanted to kiss him. I wanted to know if any of this could have the slightest chance of being real.

But that chance never came. Suddenly, I was lifted off his lap and set back down on the ground.

"She's gone," he said as he stood up from his seat. He didn't bother to give me another glance as he made his way past me and out the side door.

I stood there, trying to process what had happened. My entire body felt cold in the absence of Ethan's warmth. I wanted to call him back. I wanted to follow him. It was in this indecision that I remained rooted to my spot.

Whatever any of this meant, one thing was for sure—in this game of pretend, I was failing horribly.

The first rule of faking a relationship is you can't fall for the person you're faking it with. And from the way my heart was pounding, I was beginning to realize that this was a rule I had broken.

I was completely and utterly screwed.

Yay, me.

19

ETHAN

This was bad. This was so very, very bad.

I paced in the back storage room. I shoved my hands into my hair and tugged. Pain seared through my scalp, shocking me.

But that wasn't enough.

I needed to remind myself that this wasn't real. None of it was real.

Bea was here for a Christmas experience. She'd agreed to fake a relationship with me to help me save face around Scarlet. Any day now, she was going to leave Christmasland and never look back while I remained behind like some kicked puppy waiting for his master to return.

She was never going to come back. This wasn't her home, and I doubted she would ever want to classify it as such.

I was the idiot who was falling hard for the girl who was here for something fake. I was the idiot who allowed myself to imagine what it might be like to kiss her. To hold her. To be more to her than her fake boyfriend and Christmasland escort.

But that was not what she wanted, and she'd made that abundantly clear. To her, I was a friend. Someone she needed to help out. After she'd plopped down on my lap, I allowed myself for a nanosecond to believe that she actually wanted to touch me. But then her excuse came, and it had nothing to do with me and everything to do with my ex.

I was left in shock. The desire for what was going on between us to be real outweighed my desire to shock Scarlet. I no longer cared if she were here or not. That was the last thing on my mind. All I could think about was Bea's lips and the way she stared back at me, making me believe for a moment that she might want this as much as I did.

"Idiot," I said as I punched the rolls of toilet paper to my left. My attack left an imprint, and I knew Mom was going to ask me what happened to them, but I didn't care. I had all of this built-up tension, and it needed to go somewhere.

A soft knock sounded on the door and before I could answer, the door cracked open. My heart rate picked up at the thought that it was Bea coming to finish what we'd started, only to come crashing down when I saw that it was Scarlet. Her lips were pursed as she pushed into the room.

I let out an audible groan. Her arms were folded across her chest and she was staring me down. I quirked an eyebrow at her obvious challenge but then sighed and shut the door. She wasn't going to go anywhere until I heard her out.

I turned and leaned against a nearby rack, trying my hardest to look at ease. I took in a deep breath and then let it out. "What's up, Scar? What did you need to talk to me about so bad that you came to my mom's house to do it?"

Scarlet studied me, her expression stoic. I waited for her to respond, and it took a few seconds before she let out a soft laugh.

"I just can't get that image out of my head," she said as she flicked her hair and then reached out to fiddle with some of the complimentary soaps. "I mean, I know you like a good, hometown girl, but that chick?" She waved her hand in the direction of the living room.

I stared at her. Was she serious? That was why she wanted to talk to me, to make fun of Bea? Anger rose up inside of me. "I'm not sure why it matters who I am dating," I said. "You broke up with me, remember? You ran off with Paolo...or whatever his name is."

"Phillip?"

I waved her response away. "Yeah. Phillip."

She studied me, and then her lips slowly tipped up into a smile. "I didn't realize what I had until it was gone." She stepped forward. "You were good to me, and I took advantage of that."

I blinked at her response. She was just realizing this now? Well, wasn't that convenient.

My lack of response must have boosted her confidence. She moved even closer, and now she was only inches away. Her hand reached out, and before I could pull away, she rested it on my arm. The warmth of her fingertips rushed through me, but what had once elicited a flurry of emotions now did nothing.

I was dead to her touch.

And it felt...freeing.

I reached down and grabbed ahold of her hand. In one swift movement, I yanked it away. Her arm fell to her side, and her startled expression only empowered me more.

"You need to leave," I said as I moved to grab the door handle.

Her eyes widened. "I—"

"We're done. You wasted your time coming here. I have no interest in starting things up with you again. You and I," I said as I flicked my finger between us, "are done."

Her lips went from parted, to closed, to pinched in a matter of moments. I could see the fire burn in her gaze. The Scarlet I knew hated being told no. She hated coming in last. And she hated losing. At this moment, she was experiencing all three.

It was like staring at a volcano that was about to explode.

I didn't want to be in the same room as her when that happened. So I reached out and grabbed the door handle. I turned it and stepped out, all the while keeping my gaze fixed on Scarlet.

I'd seen enough movies to know that the enemy struck from behind. If I was going to keep myself safe, it was best to keep my focus on her until I was sure I was at a safe distance.

"Umph."

The feeling of something beneath my foot followed by two hands on my back, stopped me in my tracks. Before I could turn to see who I'd run into, Scarlet flung herself toward me. Her arms flailed as she tossed herself against my chest. The only sane thing I could do was to wrap my arms around her and hold her to my chest.

"What the heck?" I growled as I stared down at Scarlet. She was staring up at me like I hadn't just asked her to leave. She had this sappy smile on her lips and was batting her eyes as if she had something in them.

"I'm so sorry." Bea's whisper caused the hair on the back of my neck to stand up.

I straightened and turned to see her standing behind me with her eyes wide and her complexion pale. When our gazes met, she dropped hers to the ground and pinched her lips together.

Before I could utter a syllable, she turned and hurried from the hallway.

As I watched her leave, I attempted to call her back, but I couldn't get anything out. Instead, I just stood there with my brain short-circuiting as I attempted to string together a sentence that made sense.

"Well, that was easy."

Scarlet's voice brought me back to the present, and I turned to see her sappy smile had transitioned into a sinister one. Realizing that I still had my arms wrapped around her, I pushed her away and took a giant step back.

"What do you mean?" I asked as I pushed my hands through my hair. Even though I wanted to go after Bea, I wanted to make sure that Scarlet wasn't going to follow me. And I wanted to make sure that she understood I was not interested in having her near me the rest of her stay here.

Scarlet sighed as she adjusted her dress that must have been bunched up by her little stunt. When her gaze met mine once more, she looked almost bored.

"I know how to get what I want," she said as she clicked her tongue and flicked her hair. "I think I accomplished that." With those last few words, she turned and sauntered down the hall, disappearing around the corner.

I stared after her, anger and frustration rising up inside of me. Was this her whole reason for coming to Vermont? To torture me? I growled as I scrubbed my face. I, of course, had fallen right into her trap. I should have told Mom to deny her a room. I should have kept her as far away from me as possible.

Being back in the same room as her made me realize that I'd done the right thing by ejecting her from my life a few weeks ago. I was grateful that she came, only because it solidified in my mind how much I didn't want to be around her anymore. All of my moping that came from being brokenhearted was gone.

I was a new man because of her.

Not wanting to linger around any longer, I turned and headed back into the living room, where Emilia and Bea were hanging ornaments. Emilia was talking, and Bea was listening. Her expression was unreadable. I couldn't tell if she was happy or upset. Or neither.

Did it bother her that she saw me with Scarlet? Was it ridiculous of me to hope that she cared enough about me to be affected by seeing us?

And then guilt settled in. If she did feel bad about seeing us, did that mean she was hurting? That wasn't what I wanted. The desire to make sure she was okay overcame me, so I hurried over to her and grabbed a small wood nativity ornament from the box. It had no hook, so I moved over to the bundle of hooks on the chair cushion next to the tree.

"Oh, you're joining us now?" Emilia asked.

I turned to face her. She looked a little peeved as she stood there with her hands on her hips. I threaded the hook through the ornament's eyelet and nodded. "I figured you guys needed the help."

Emilia's scowl deepened. "What about Scarlet? Where did she go?"

I glanced toward the stairs. I hoped Scarlet had disappeared up them, so she could pack her bags and return to Chicago. "I'm guessing home." I shrugged. "But I honestly don't care where she went."

I turned so I was facing Bea. She was turning a snowflake ornament around in her hands. "We're definitely over. Whatever you saw, it wasn't what you think. I told her to leave, and she fell into my arms." I winced at how that explanation sounded. But it was the truth, so I stuck with it.

Bea's cheeks turned rosy as she brought her gaze up. "Really?" she asked.

I nodded and reached down to retrieve an ornament hook. Then I handed it over to her. "I swear. Scarlet and I are over, and there is no chance of us ever getting back together."

Bea took the hook from me, all the while pinching her lips as if she weren't sure what to say. Then slowly, a smile emerged, and she looked up at me through her long lashes. I could see the hope in her gaze, and that only made my heart pound that much harder. I'd remedied the issue that had come between us, which meant we might be able to move forward with whatever it was we had.

One thing I knew for sure was that Bea cared about me. Her reaction told me that things between us went deeper than just her desire for a Christmasland experience. That, perhaps, we were more real than fake.

And that thought gave me the first glimmer of hope I'd felt in a long time.

That thought made me believe, for the first time, in the power of Christmas.

20

BEATRICE

"Everybody count with me," Em shouted to the few guests lingering in the living room. Some were talking in hushed tones. An elderly couple was putting together a puzzle. None of them seemed interested in joining in with us as we counted down.

Em stood there with the plug and an extension cord and a really ridiculously happy grin on her face. She looked like a kid in a candy store as she stood there smiling.

"Three," she cheered.

A woman drinking some hot cocoa was startled, and the brown liquid sloshed in her mug.

I pressed my fingers to my lips, hoping to get Em to keep it down, but she didn't look the least bit interested in acknowledging me. Instead, she called out, "Two."

Realizing how happy my friend was and not wanting to be a killjoy, I clapped my hands.

"One," I cheered with her. She dramatically plugged in the lights of the tree.

They flickered for a moment before they went out. A collective "Aww" sounded through the room, which only lasted for a moment until the lights flickered back on and stayed.

A cheer sounded from Em, me, Ethan, and Porter, which was soon joined by the rest of the guests. Either they were just as excited that the lights were on as we were, or they were just grateful for this all to be over with.

I peeked over at Ethan, who was smiling as he stared at the tree. After our little hallway debacle, he'd come back and was actually present. He helped hang the ornaments and placed the star at the top. There were even a few times that I caught him smiling.

And more often than not, when he was smiling, it was because he was staring at me.

It caused heat to prick my neck and, I was fairly sure, a blush to tint my skin. If he didn't think I liked him before, I couldn't imagine him doubting that now.

Wanting to talk, I took one big step forward, so I was right next to him. My arm brushed his, and I waited for him to pull back, but he didn't. Instead, he glanced down at me and his mysterious smile emerged.

"You look happy," I said as I wiggled my finger in his direction.

Ethan shrugged. "Could it be..." He tapped his finger with his chin and then wiggled his eyebrows. "That I am happy?"

I raised my eyebrows. "Wow. The grinch's heart really can grow." I leaned forward with a pretend magnifying glass aimed at his chest. "What did that feel like?"

He chuckled. "Do you mean to tell me that you don't feel it too?"

I straightened and glanced around. "What?" I whispered. "The magic of Christmas?"

He nodded. "Yeah. I mean, I've been a skeptic. But this year, things are different." His expression stilled as if he wanted me to feel what he was saying. "Is it different for you?"

As much as I wanted to deny it, I did feel it. Obvious and

strong and deep in my bones. He had an effect on me that I hadn't felt in a long time. He made me feel...hopeful.

I met his gaze, and for a moment, I wanted to agree with him. I wanted to jump into a relationship with him with both feet and a determination that I was desperate to have. I wanted to throw away the thoughts of fear that lingered in my mind and just feel.

"Is it real?" I asked before I could stop myself.

Ethan frowned. "Is what real?"

Feeling as if I'd just peeled back my protective layer and exposed my fear, I raised my hands to the room around me. "This. What I'm feeling."

He paused for a moment, and he searched my gaze as if he was wondering exactly the same thing. Not wanting to hide behind my pain anymore, I offered him a small smile. He held my gaze and then nodded.

"Yes."

The world around me began to soften. All of my fear that my experiences in Christmasland were concocted to give me a Hallmark experience floated away, and all I was left with were the feelings that were growing inside of my chest.

The feelings I had for Ethan.

Slowly and cautiously, I lowered my hand and inched it closer to his. Just when I was certain that he wasn't going to take it, the feeling of his warm hand engulfing mine washed over me. I threaded my fingers through his, and he squeezed my hand.

"Well, look at you two," Em said as she sauntered up to us. She had two mugs in her hands and handed one of them to me. "No holiday creamer as usual," she said.

I thanked her and took it with my free hand. There was no way I wanted to let Ethan's hand go. Not when it felt so right to hold it.

"Hey, it's not so strange. Ethan doesn't like it either."

Em was halfway to handing the other mug to Ethan when she paused and narrowed her eyes. Then she glanced down at the coffee. "Ah, well, then you're not going to like this," she said as she took a sip.

I chuckled, and Ethan nodded. "Yeah, I probably won't."

Em kept the mug at her lips as she glanced between us. After another sip, she pulled back. "You two are like a match made in heaven, aren't you?" she asked. She dabbed at her lips.

Embarrassment heated my insides. The last thing I needed was for my friend to make a big deal of things.

Ethan just shrugged. "I guess so."

My smile deepened as I stepped closer to him. I liked Ethan. I liked him a lot.

"It's almost like it's...too good of a match." I didn't like Em's tone. She had a skeptical look in her eyes that I hadn't seen the entire time we were here.

"Hey," I hissed. Why was she acting like this? I was finally happy, and she had to snow on my parade like that?

Em threaded her arm through mine and squeezed it tight. Then she nodded toward the stairs. "Can I talk to you in private for a minute?"

I wanted to stay right where I was, but I knew if I didn't go, I was just going to spend the evening fighting off my best friend's stares. It was better to address her concerns now before her suspicions grew deeper. I could tell that they were already rooted deep, and it was going to take some pulling to get them out.

I slipped my hand from Ethan's. "I'll be right back," I said as I dragged Em out into the foyer.

Once we were out of earshot, I turned to face her. "What? What is it? What could it possibly be?"

My outburst must have startled her because she blinked as she pulled back. Realizing that I sounded like a crazy person, I took in a deep breath and closed my eyes. "Sorry. I didn't mean to snap."

Em shook her head. "It's fine. That's what happens when you are wound a bit too tight."

I glared at her and then sighed. "What did you need to talk to me about?"

Em took a painfully slow sip of her coffee and then lowered her mug and set it on the small table next to us. She folded her arms. "What's going on with you and Ethan?"

"What?"

The crease between Em's eyebrows grew, and I could tell that she was worried about something. That made my frustration with her lessen a bit. After all, she always had my best interests at heart. Why would that change now?

But I also wasn't sure how to answer her question. What were Ethan and I doing? At this moment, I wasn't completely sure, and for the first time, I was okay with that. All I wanted was to spend time with him, learning and discovering everything about him.

So I shrugged and fiddled with a snag on my sleeve. "I don't know. We're just…feeling things out?"

Em pinched the bridge of her nose as she took in a deep breath. She was holding her true feelings back and that worried me. I didn't want her to feel as if she couldn't tell me what she was thinking. We'd always been honest with each other since the formation of our friendship. Why would we stop now?

"I have no intention of seeing Porter when we leave Christmasland," she said slowly as she pulled her hand down from her face.

I studied her. In a way, I already knew that. But there were times when I'd wondered if something had happened between them. If they were faking things, they were good at faking.

"What?" I asked, hoping she'd clarify her words.

Em sighed. "I'm here for the experience. And I know you think that the town isn't out to give their guests a Hallmark experience, but it's true." She leaned her shoulder against the wall and folded her arms. "Porter is an actor."

I blinked. "What?"

"Porter. He's not some rich guy from the city. He's an actor." She said the last word slowly, drawing out every syllable.

"An actor?"

Em nodded. "He's here to play the part of a rich guy in a small town."

"How do you know that?" My entire body went cold as I stood there. It was fake? It had all been fake? And I was the idiot who fell for it?

"I overheard him talking to his agent." She paused and wrinkled her nose. "Begging was more like it. He's out of work and needs the money." She shrugged. "When he got off the phone, I confronted him. He confessed to it all." She waved her hand in the direction of the kitchen. "Carol is paying him to pretend."

Tears pricked my eyelids as her words settled deep in my chest. This was all an act. Which meant Ethan was just playing a part as well.

Em pushed off the wall and closed the gap between us. She wrapped her arms around me and pulled me close. "I wanted you to know before you got in too deep. I don't know what Ethan's intentions are, and I want to tell you that they are honorable...but I'm just not sure."

I nodded as tears threatened to fall. I didn't want to break down in the hallway. Not with everyone around asking me what was wrong. I didn't want to be known as the idiotic girl who fell for the experience.

"Everything okay?" Ethan's voice was low.

Desperate to not have him see me cry, I quickly wiped at my cheeks and took in a deep breath before I turned around. I wasn't going to let Ethan know that I was confused about our relationship. In fact, I was going to give him the benefit of the doubt. He could be just as lost as I was, and maybe, he actually was being honest in the way he was treating me.

Maybe he wanted to be around me instead of being forced to be with me. I could hold out hope, couldn't I?

"Yes," I whispered as I picked up my coffee and took a sip. The warm liquid helped ground me and stilled my raging storm of emotions. I wasn't going to jump to conclusions, and I wouldn't act until I was certain of Ethan's apathy toward me.

"We'll talk more later," I whispered to Em. She just nodded and gave me a small smile. I appreciated her concern for me, but I was going to make my own decisions for now. I was going to hold onto a glimmer of hope that things between Ethan and I were real.

After all, what other choice did I have?

When I stepped up to Ethan, he gave me a small smile. I could tell that he was hesitant about something, but I wasn't sure what it was. "You okay?" he asked.

I chewed on my bottom lip, Em's words still rolling around in my mind. I shook my head slightly. I wasn't going to worry about that right now. If Ethan gave me a reason to doubt what he was doing for me, then I would allow myself to digest what she'd said.

Sure, Porter may be a plant, but that didn't mean Ethan was.

"Yes," I said softly as my entire body moved to protect my heart. The last thing I needed was for another man to break it. I had a sinking suspicion that if he did, I was never going to be the same.

We walked into the living room, where Carol was seated at the piano. She was playing Christmas songs, and a crowd had gathered around to start singing.

Ethan moved to stand closer to me, his arm brushing against mine. Shivers erupted across my skin, and my heart quickened in response. It angered me that I was so easily swayed by the presence of this man. After all, we'd only just met, and yet I'd somehow deluded myself into thinking there was something between us.

So what if he was an actor planted at the inn to give me the quintessential Christmas experience? If he was, he was doing a dang good job. For a moment there, he'd convinced me that he cared about me.

For a moment there, I'd believed I cared for him.

And from the way my heart was aching, I knew that even if Ethan was playing a part, I wasn't. His script might tell him to care for me, but mine didn't.

The feelings I had were real, and no matter how much I tried to convince myself otherwise, it didn't matter.

I liked Ethan. Period.

Crap.

21

ETHAN

Bea was acting strange. After Emilia asked her into the hallway, I went after them to make sure everything was okay. When I got to them, I could tell something had happened. Bea was upset, and I wasn't sure why.

When we got back into the living room and stood off to the side of the piano, I could tell something was different. Bea was different.

I glanced down at her and gave her a soft smile. She didn't acknowledge me. Instead, she kept her gaze focused on Mom. She slowly clapped her hands as she sang *"We Wish You a Merry Christmas."* I wanted to find the desire to sing, but it was sorely lacking. All I could do was drag my gaze away from Bea and over to Mom, who was studying me with a confused expression.

I shrugged, hoping that would give her enough of an explanation as to what was going on, but she didn't seem like she believed me at all. Instead, she doubled down on her stare as she tipped her head in Bea's direction.

What did she want from me?

Realizing that Mom wasn't going to stop staring at me, I lifted my hands and began clapping and singing. That seemed to appease Mom, and her rigid expression softened. I hated that she felt that the best way to give Bea a good experience was for me to be someone I wasn't.

Because this whole Christmas charade wasn't me. None of it was.

I wanted to be able to talk to Bea like I would normally. I wanted to take her out and eat dinner with her without the pressure of working in some Christmas cliché. Why couldn't Mom just back off and let me be me?

I had reason to hope that Bea would like the real me. We had similar tastes and an equal apathy toward this holiday. I mean, sure, the more time I spent in Christmasland, the more I was beginning to see the magic of Christmas. But that didn't mean that I shared my mom's unhealthy obsession. It meant that I would enjoy it for the week leading up to Christmas.

And for me, that was saying a lot.

Mom started up *"Joy to the World,"* and I'd had enough singing to last me a lifetime, so I nudged Bea. She startled and glanced up at me. I offered her an apologetic smile and nodded toward the entryway. "Wanna get out of here?"

Her eyes widened as she studied me for a moment and then nodded. "Sure."

I wasn't a fan of her hesitation, but if she was willing to escape, I was one hundred percent on board. Once I got her away from the crowd, I'd ask her what was wrong. And I hoped that she would feel comfortable enough to let me in.

I grabbed a hold of her hand as I led her through the crowd of people and into the dining room. A few guests were still eating Mom's evening snacks, so I kept my hand firmly wrapped around Bea's as I pulled her into the kitchen. I wanted privacy, and this was the only place to get it.

Once we were inside and the door swung shut, I waited to see what Bea would do with her hand. A few seconds ticked by before she wiggled her fingers free and headed over to the sink. She turned the water on.

"I'm parched," she said as she began to pull open the cupboards in search of a glass.

It was going to take her awhile. Mom's kitchen reflected her personality—scattered and nonsensical. I pulled out a glass and walked over to hold it under the water.

This brought me inches from Bea, and suddenly, all I wanted was to be closer to her. To pull her into my arms and kiss her like I'd wanted to do all day. Like I'd wanted to do earlier before we were interrupted by Mom.

I didn't hold back as I stared down at Bea. Her cheeks were flushed, and her attention focused on the water as it filled the glass. I wanted her to look at me. I was certain she would see how I felt for her if she did. She would understand that I wanted to be closer to her than anything else.

She would know that Scarlet meant nothing to me.

"Bea," I whispered.

Her body tensed as I stepped closer to her. A flash of fear rushed over me as I saw her hesitation. She was worried about something, and I wasn't sure what. I wanted her to be open with me, but something was holding her back.

Water began to rush over my fingers. I glanced down to see that I'd overfilled the glass. I reached out to turn off the water, and Bea took that moment to step away from me.

I tried to not let it bother me. I tipped the glass over to let some of the water out and then handed it to Bea. She sniffled and brushed her wrist against her nose as she glanced around.

"Tissue?" she asked.

I scanned the room. When I came up empty-handed, I nodded towards Mom's office. "I'm sure some are in there." When I stepped forward, she held her hand up. It brushed my arm and caused me to freeze.

"I can get it," she whispered.

I wanted to fight her. I wanted to tell her that it really was no problem, but she was already halfway across the kitchen before I could get the words out. So I found a dish towel, dried off my hand, and settled in against the countertop.

Things felt strained between us, and I was trying hard not to read into that. Instead, I was going to focus on the fact that she was here and willing to be around me. I was determined to show her the kind of person I really was, sans Christmasland.

When she didn't come back right away, I straightened and peered toward the office. Did she get lost in there? Was it that hard to find the tissues?

Seconds ticked by, and she didn't emerge. Wondering what was going on, I walked over to the doorway to find Bea standing over Mom's desk, staring at something.

I furrowed my brow. "Everything okay?"

Bea jumped away from Mom's desk with a few pieces of paper in her hand. She held them out to me. "What are these?" she asked.

Confused, I reached forward and took them from her. One glance and my heart sank. "Bingo cards," I whispered. Not only bingo cards, but crossed off bingo cards. Apparently, Mom had been tracking what Bea and I were doing.

I glanced up to see Bea wipe a tear away. She kept her gaze focused on the ground. "I can explain," I said as I saw her body stiffen. She was getting ready to sprint from the room.

"It was all a lie, wasn't it?" she asked. My heart broke as she turned her gaze upwards to meet mine. I could see hurt and betrayal in her eyes.

"No, it wasn't." How could I get her to understand that it was never a lie for me?

"It wasn't?" She pulled the papers from my hands. "A Christmas morning breakfast. A sleigh ride. Chopping down a tree. An older girlfriend. A grumpy hero?" She waved the paper in my face. "This is exactly what you planned for me. Am I right?"

I slowly nodded. The ability to form words left me, and all I could do was stand there.

Bea stared at me and then back down at the paper. "Are you going to tell me that you are royal next? Or that you need my help planning a Christmas ball?" She crumpled up the paper and tossed it into the garbage next to her. "I thought you did those things because you cared about me. But it's all a lie."

A tear escaped, and she angrily wiped it away. "You. Carol. Porter. You all lied to me and Em." She sniffed as she studied the ground. She took in a deep breath and glanced up at me. "Why? Why would you do that to us?" Her voice drifted down to a whisper. "To me?"

I had to tell her that it wasn't true. I used the bingo cards as a template of the things I could do for her, but I wanted to do them. I wanted to spend that time with her. But I feared she wouldn't believe me. My words would fall on deaf ears, and all she would hear was betrayal. I didn't want to rub salt in her wounds.

"I'm sorry," I whispered. I wasn't sure what else to say. I'd betrayed her. I'd lied to her. Even if I wanted to tell myself it was for a good cause, the truth was I'd led her on. Just like Scarlet did to me.

Bea studied me. She worried her lips as her eyes filled with tears. "Is that all?"

I nodded. What else could I do? I'd walked away from Scarlet. If Bea wanted to walk away, did I have any right to try to stop her? If I cared about her, should I just let her go?

"So it was all a lie? Up on the rooftop? The baking contest? The kiss?"

I winced. Every one of those experiences had been real. Those were the moments that I revealed who I really was. But how could I tell her that those were true when she was so convinced that everything was a lie?

"I wanted to do those things for you. The rooftop was my

secret hiding place when I was a kid. You won that contest fair and square. And the kiss" —I swallowed— "I wanted..."

"I'll be right back with more sugar cookies, Dale." Mom's voice preceded her as she stepped into the kitchen. The door swung on its hinges behind her as she turned toward the office. I could see her confusion as she noticed us.

"What are you two doing in here?" she asked.

Bea didn't look interested in sticking around. She had her arms wrapped around her chest, and she looked as if she was doing everything she possibly could to protect herself. "I'm going to go," she said as she sidestepped Mom.

"Beatrice," Mom called out, but that didn't stop her. She was through the kitchen door and out into the dining room in a flash.

Mom looked confused as she stared at me. "What happened?"

I crumpled up the bingo sheets and tossed them in the trash. Anger. Frustration. Pain. All of it was rising up inside of me. I turned to face Mom. "She found out. She put two and two together and realized what we were trying to do. That this was all fake." I waved my hands to signify that "*this*" was the inn, the town, and lastly, me.

Mom's eyebrows shot up. "Fake?"

I nodded as I walked past her and over to the back door, where I shoved my feet into my boots. I needed to get out of here. I needed to get some fresh air and clear my head.

"But it wasn't fake," Mom said as she trailed after me.

I turned to study her. "What are you talking about?"

Mom rested her hands on her hips. "I saw the way you looked at that girl. I'm sorry, but there is no actor in this world who can conjure up that kind of intensity." She waggled her finger at me. "You care about the girl. Sure, we may have manufactured the experience, but the feelings were real."

I stared at her. I knew that. Why was she telling me?

I grabbed my coat from the hook and shoved my arms into the sleeves. "It doesn't matter, though. She doesn't care."

Mom parted her lips, but before she could say anything, I yanked open the back door. The cold wind pierced my skin, and I shrunk deeper into my coat.

"Ethan," Mom said as she moved to stop me.

I held up my hand. "It doesn't matter anymore. It's over."

I didn't want to hear what else she had to say. I gave her a quick nod and headed down the back stairs and out into the dark, snowy wonderland.

At least out here, I could clear my head. Out here, I could make sense of what just happened.

Out here, I could lick the wounds of my broken heart.

22

BEATRICE

"Wait. What are we doing?" Em asked as she stood in the closet doorway, staring at me as I threw my clothes into my suitcase.

It had been exactly five minutes since I stormed out of the kitchen, and I was ready to get the heck out of here. Em seemed more confused than anything. I'd pulled her away from Porter and dragged her upstairs. Now she was staring at me, waiting for an explanation that I wasn't quite ready to give.

I knew she would never say *I told you so*, but that didn't stop the words from playing on repeat in my mind. The truth was, she did tell me. And the even harder truth was, I didn't listen.

I'd fallen for Ethan, and now I was the idiot with a broken heart as realization bore down on me. Everything had been fake. Everything.

Even now, my heart was trying to tell me that parts had been real. It wanted me to hope that I had been right about some things. For example, Ethan's feelings for me. They had to be real, right?

I mean, I'd seen my share of movies, and actors could do many things. But making the audience believe that they truly loved their costar was not one of them. Ethan had done that for me. He'd made me stupidly and ridiculously believe that he cared about me.

Man, I was an idiot.

I grabbed my jeans and shoved them into my suitcase. They were in a ball instead of folded like I normally packed them, but I didn't care. I needed to get out of here.

Em sighed and folded her arms. "I'm not going to be able to talk you out of this, am I?" she asked.

I shook my head. "Nope. Might as well get on board."

She studied me for a moment longer before she nodded and walked past me to grab her suitcase. Then she laid it on the ground and opened it up.

We were packed and ready to go within fifteen minutes. Thankfully, Em didn't push me for an explanation. Instead, we gathered our things in silence. I knew she had questions, but she kept them to herself, which I was grateful for. I'd had enough of the ridiculous tears that were poised to spill any second, and if I was forced to talk about Ethan, I knew they would come tumbling down.

And I couldn't have that.

Not right now.

When I got home, I could let the sobs out and let the tears flow. But I had a few hours before that could happen.

Once everything was packed, I pulled open the door to find Carol's worried smile on the other side. She had her hand raised as if she were just about to knock. Her gaze slipped down to my suitcase and then back up to me, where her expression faltered.

"You're leaving?" she asked.

I nodded. "Yes." I didn't know what to say. I was disappointed that she let this happen, but I wasn't angry—not like I was with Ethan. With Carol, I expected something like this. But I trusted Ethan, and he broke that trust.

She worried her lips. "Is there anything I can say to change your mind?"

I sighed and shook my head. "No. I'm just ready to get back to normal life." I gave her a weak smile, hoping that was all it would take for her to leave me alone.

She glanced from me to Em. "I'm so sorry," she whispered. "I must have been out of my mind to arrange any of this." Her voice trailed off. "I just wanted you two to have a great experience and for you to finally have a real Christmas. I guess I didn't think that arranging things for you to do was the exact opposite of real."

It was so hard to be angry at a woman who looked like Mrs. Claus. As much as I wanted to be frustrated with her, it just wasn't coming. Instead, I felt sorry for her. She had unrealistic expectations when it came to this holiday, and I didn't like the fact that I was the one bringing light to that expectation.

I reached forward and gave her a big hug. "It's okay," I said as I pulled back. "You did a great job. I just need to get home."

Carol studied me. I could see all of her questions in her gaze, but I wasn't in the mood to hear any of them. I was ready to go.

"Are you sure? I'm confident that we can come up with a better solution for all of this." She waved her hand toward my luggage.

"No. I need to go."

Em gave Carol a smile and a wave. "It was fun. You did a great job."

I gave her a smile as well and tried to follow Em to the stairs only to be stopped by Carol. She grabbed hold of my arm, halting my escape. I glanced down to see her earnest gaze peering up at me.

"Don't hate Ethan. He was doing me a favor. This is all my fault. I wanted you to have a good experience, and he wasn't on board at first. But after a while, he decided that he wanted you to have a good Christmas, too." I could see her tears brimming, and it made my heart ache even more.

I hated that she was hurting because of this as well.

I patted her hand. "I don't hate Ethan." And there was truth to that. I didn't hate the man. In fact, I think I cared for him more that I realized. I just wasn't ready to have yet another Christmas ruined. Not in the most Christmassy place in the world. How could I ruin the holiday when everything around me was manufactured to make it perfect?

Carol sighed. "That's good. 'Cause I'm fairly certain he loves you."

I stopped. My entire body freezing to the spot. "He what?"

Carol studied me. "He cares about you. A lot. I've never seen him step out of his comfort zone for a woman like he did with you. Ethan wasn't lying when he told you he doesn't like Christmas. He really doesn't." She patted my hand. "But he started caring when you came around. I think that speaks volumes."

Warmth spread throughout my body like hot chocolate on a cold day. I stared at Carol as I processed her words. "He wanted to trick me?"

Carol wrinkled her nose. "I wouldn't stay tricked. He wanted to give you the kind of Christmas you should have had as a kid." She smiled up at me. "That's what we all wanted."

I felt like a jerk. A giant pile of coal. Here I was, complaining because the people around me wanted to give me the best Christmas ever. How could I have been so selfish? And Ethan...

I swallowed hard against the lump in my throat. I was so rude to him. He was shocked, I could see it in his gaze. He wanted to tell me the truth, but I just jumped to conclusions.

"I like him too," I whispered. I liked him a lot.

"Really?" Carol's lips parted into an *o* as she stared at me. Then she shook her head. "Can you tell him that? 'Cause I think he is under the impression that you hate him. He stormed from the house, and I'm not sure where he went."

"He left?" I glanced toward the hallway window to see that it was pitch-black outside. The truth was, I wanted to see him again. I wanted to tell him how I felt.

Carol nodded. "Yes."

I glanced back at Em, who shrugged. "We're still waiting for the car to be dropped off. You have some time to go find him."

I chewed my lip. I wasn't sure if it was wise to go after him when he obviously wanted to brood alone in the cold. But what if something happened to him? I'd never forgive myself.

I set my bags down and turned to Carol. "Where do you think he went?"

Carol's eyes widened. "I'm not sure."

I held up my phone to show Em. "Call me if he comes back here. I'll go looking for him."

Before either of them could stop me, I was rushing down the stairs. I ran over to the coat rack, where I pulled my jacket down and shoved my arms into it. Then I pulled the door open and dashed out into the cold. The wind whipped around me, causing me to squint against the dancing snow.

I rounded the house and started toward the back. I found a path that looked as if it had been recently used and followed it into the woods. Thoughts of being murdered in the dark woods flooded my mind, but I kept those fears at bay as I hummed Christmas carols under my breath.

I was going to be fine. I was.

Ten minutes passed, and I was now firmly convinced that I was never going to find Ethan and that I was going to die out here. Just as hopelessness filled my chest, the path opened up to a clearing centered on a gazebo. Small twinkle lights shone against the darkness, and I raised my hand up to shield my eyes.

Was this heaven? Had I died?

A dark shadow moved inside the gazebo, and my heart began to pound. Nope. I hadn't died yet. But I was about to. The shadow was moving straight toward me.

"Beatrice?"

My murderer sounded a lot like Ethan.

Just then, I stepped forward and must have found a dip in the grass because my foot twisted and I fell into the snow in slow motion. I put my hands out to brace myself, and thankfully, snow was a soft substance to fall on. Feeling embarrassed, I attempted to stand, only to have a sharp pain radiate through my foot. I fell back into the snow.

"Are you okay?" Ethan's panicked voice drew my attention up to find him hovering over me.

"Yeah, I'm fine." Why did things always have to happen this way? Why was he constantly coming to my rescue?

Before I could stop him, he had both arms wrapped around me and was lifting me up. He held me to his chest as he brought me to the gazebo and set me down on one of the benches inside. Kneeling in front of me, he gingerly picked up my foot.

"Why did you come out here?" he growled as he inspected my ankle.

I watched him, my heart filling with a peace that I hadn't felt in a very long time. Despite what he had or hadn't done, Carol was right. Ethan cared about me, and I cared about him. And that was all that mattered.

"Was Scarlet really your ex?"

He paused and then went back to unlacing my shoe. "Yes." Once it was loose enough, he carefully pulled it off.

"Did she come here on her own?"

His hands were warm against my foot. The feeling of his touch sent shockwaves through my system.

"Yes." He paused as if he were waiting for me to ask another question.

Emotions clung to my throat as I prepared myself to ask the last question that I needed to know the answer to. The one that would determine if I stayed or if I left.

"Did you want to spend time with me?" The words left my lips in a whisper. When he didn't answer, I feared that the wind had picked them up and took them away before he could hear them.

He straightened and turned to face me. Suddenly, he was

right there, caging me between his chest and the bench I was sitting on. I didn't even notice that my foot had fallen to rest against the outside of his boot. All I could feel was the heat in his gaze.

His gaze trailed down to my lips and then back up to hold my gaze as if he never wanted to let it go. "Yes, I wanted to spend time with you. Those ridiculous bingo cards were just a template for things we could do. Everything I said, everything I felt was real." He reached up and cradled my cheek in his hand. "This is real."

Tears filled my eyes as I allowed myself to lean into his hand. He must have taken that as permission because, a moment later, his hand was on my chin and he was tipping my face toward his.

Our lips met, and I felt my breath catch in my throat. He was so warm and inviting that I almost feared we'd made a mistake. What if he realized that he'd made a mistake?

He growled as if he'd read my mind, and suddenly, his arm was wrapped around my back as he pulled me closer to him. I pushed fear from my mind and wrapped my arms around his neck and deepened the kiss.

Every part of me wanted to feel every part of him. I wanted to bring myself closer to him in a way that I hadn't wanted to do with any man. Ethan was different. Ethan was special.

It didn't matter that we were sitting in a gazebo completely open to the elements. It didn't matter that I was shivering as we kissed. I was exactly where I needed to be.

Ethan pulled back and studied me. I could see the worry in his gaze. I shook my head, but my chattering teeth told a different story.

"You're freezing," he said as he shook off his jacket and wrapped it around me.

"I'm fine."

He furrowed his brow. "Let's make a promise not to lie to each other ever again."

I studied him and then sighed. "Fine. I'm freezing, but I don't want this to end."

Ethan leaned forward and brushed his lips against mine. "Who said this was the ending?"

I wrapped my arms around him as he pulled me back to his chest. "It's not?"

He leaned down so I could grab my shoe and then pulled me close. I could feel the warmth of his chest as it cascaded down my body. I didn't need a heated house, I just needed Ethan next to me.

"Definitely not the end."

I snuggled into his neck and sighed. "Really?"

He nodded. "Really."

I leaned forward and pressed my lips to his once more. He chuckled as he pulled back so that he could turn off the lights in the gazebo and carefully walk down the stairs. Then he turned to stare into my eyes with an intensity that I'd never experienced before.

His lips tipped up into a smile as he rested his forehead on mine. "I'd say this is just the beginning."

I tightened my grip on him, bringing myself closer to his ear. I allowed my cheek to linger against his as I whispered, "I agree."

He pulled back and kissed me again. This time, he didn't let up. The passion I felt in his embrace took my breath away. And I was fine with that. Because I felt the same.

With all the promises that Christmasland guaranteed, I never expected to find the one person who made me want to stay. Who made me feel whole.

And I found all of that in Ethan.

I found my Christmas spirit.

I found myself.

"I love you," I whispered, breaking the kiss.

He nodded. "I love you, too."

EPILOGUE

Beatrice

"Hurry! Sit down. It's starting," Em called out from the living room.

I was elbow-deep in popcorn in the kitchen, and we were sitting down to watch the Hallmark movie marathon on Christmas Eve. Apparently, that was a tradition here at the North Pole. Popcorn and all the Christmas sap one could want.

Ethan popped his head out from Carol's office and waved a stack of papers at me. "I've got the bingo cards."

I laughed. After all, it's better to embrace the pain than run from it. "Are they good?"

He nodded. "The guests will like them. Plus, Mom is giving a free vacation next Christmas to the winner."

I slipped some popcorn into my mouth. "Brilliant."

Ethan took that moment to kiss me. When he pulled back, I swallowed and glowered at him. "We need to set some kissing ground rules," I said.

He shrugged. "I'm just making up for the fact that I failed in the kitchen last time."

I chuckled and watched as he pulled a piece of paper from his pocket. He hesitated and then handed it to me. "Here."

Confused, I began to unfold it. Printed on the paper was a bingo card that was partially filled out.

"What is this?" I scanned the paper. *Snow ball fight. Misunderstanding. Interrupted first kiss.*

"This is the bingo card I actually used."

I parted my lips as I glanced from the card back to him. *"The* card?"

He nodded. "I thought you should have it."

I chuckled as I set it reverently down on the counter behind me. Then I turned and wrapped my arms around him. "I love it," I whispered, my lips tipped toward his ears.

His arms wrapped around me, and he pulled me close. Then his lips found mine, and we kissed like we should have kissed the last time we stood in this room.

"Oh, you two. Everyone is waiting for you," Carol said as she hurried to the fridge and grabbed the container of fudge we'd made early that day.

Ethan and I pulled apart, and I offered her a sheepish smile. "Sorry about that."

Carol laughed as she turned and gave me a one-armed hug. "Don't ever apologize for caring about my son. I'm just happy you two have found your missing Christmas spirit." She leaned in. "I think this is just what Christmasland needed. And more importantly, I think this is just what you needed."

I nodded and watched her hurry from the room. Ethan followed after her with the stack of papers in his hand and a wink in my direction.

Now alone, I folded my arms across my chest and sighed. Carol was right. Christmasland was exactly what I needed. Not only did it help me believe in magic again, but my writer's block had lifted. I'd been able to write ten thousand words over the last few days.

Who would have guessed that all I needed to jumpstart my life was a town like this? A place where Christmas lives forever and where the wildest dreams come true.

I grabbed the giant bowl of popcorn and headed into the living room. Thankfully, Ethan had saved me a spot, and I snuggled in next to him. The movie began to play, and I felt Ethan press his lips to the top of my head. My heart settled into a satisfied murmur as I leaned into him.

"Merry Christmas," I whispered.

He nodded and dropped his lips down to my ear. "Merry Christmas."

***

If you're in the mood for MORE Christmas romance, head on
over to Amazon and grab them ALL!
Forgiving the Billionaire
HERE
Winter at Christmas Inn
HERE
Second Chance Mistletoe Kisses
HERE

If you love friendship stories with a mixture of romance, check
out my Women's Fiction series, The Red Stiletto Book Club seres.
HERE

I also has a fabulous Family Saga series.
Start book 1, Coming Home to Honey Grove,
HERE!

Join my Newsletter!
Find great deals on my books and other sweet romance!
Get, Fighting Love for the Cowboy FREE

just for signing up!
Grab it HERE!

SHE'S AN IRS AUDITOR DESPERATE TO PROVE HERSELF.
HE'S A COWBOY TRYING TO HOLD ONTO HIS RANCH.
LOVE WAS NOT ON THE AGENDA.

If you want to connect with me, head on over to website for a list
of my books.
HERE

I love to connect with you on my social media platforms:

Facebook
Instagram
TikTok

Made in the USA
Columbia, SC
17 December 2020